Part 1

The Escape

Chapter 1

Lav rolled in the shredded newspaper. A piece stuck to the fur on his back. He stretched his neck and tried to nip it off. Something ran past him. He saw a blur of green fur, then the paper was gone.

Lav sat up. Kama stood near him, wagging her tail, the paper in her mouth.

"Too slow," she said, before running further away.

Lav yelped and chased after Kama. She ran past the rest of the puppies, lying in a pile. That's all the others seemed to do these days, sleep.

Kama ran around the pen three times before he trapped her in a corner.

"You're in trouble now," Lav said. He pounced on Kama and bit her neck. Not a hard bite, a playful one, the kind dogs give when they're wrestling with a friend.

Kama nipped him back. She forgot about the paper, which fell from her mouth back to the floor. The two pulled at each other's ears and tumbled beside the metal bars that imprisoned them.

Kama stopped. She sat up and stared at the door.

"What is it?" Lav asked.

Kama held her ears higher than normal. "Someone's coming."

Lav listened. He couldn't hear anything, but he did see Cryp lift his head from the top of the puppy pile. Cryp always slept on top.

"Food," Kama said.

Cryp must have heard it too. He hopped off the other sleeping puppies, ran to the empty bowls lying by the front of the cage, and barked. Kama and Lav also ran to the front.

Cryp and Kama were always the first to know if someone was coming to the room. They had a lot of other things in common too. They were colored the same, each having patches of green, black, and brown on their fur. They were the only dogs in the room with more than one color on their coat. The others were solid colors. Two were blue, two were green, two red, two orange, two yellow, and Lav was a purple dog along with Violetta.

Sometimes the humans with white coats took Cryp and Kama out of the pen. They even brought them outside. Lav didn't understand what it meant to be outside. He only knew that Kama wagged her tail every time the humans came to get her. Sometimes, she even yelped and ran to the front of the cage to greet them.

While outside, the humans played games with her and Cryp. The humans liked to hide things. If Cryp or Kama could smell where something was hidden and sit next to it, they would get a treat.

It made Lav jealous. He wanted the humans with white coats to play games with him too. They usually ignored him. Whenever someone did pick him up, it was to poke him with a needle. Lav learned to growl and bark if they came close. He used to bite too. He still tried to bite, but they had learned to hold his mouth shut while forcing him onto the table.

Lav turned his head to the side. He could finally hear wheels rolling down the hallway. Eventually, a man, pushing a supply cart, came through the door. He had dark hair, except for a few areas of gray near the temples. The man seemed to wear the same dark blue clothes each day. A large ring of keys hung from his belt, jingling as he worked.

The others woke up. Soon all fourteen puppies were barking and pawing at the pen's bars. Lav smelled the bucket of dog food on the cart. It made his tail wag harder.

"Hello little ones," the man said. "You have so much energy today!"

This man usually talked to the puppies, something the people in white coats never did. Lav couldn't tell what he was saying, but knew his words were gentle. This human was also the only one who fed them, cleaned, and sprinkled fresh paper around the pen. He was the only person that Lav was fond of: the only human he trusted.

Chapter 2

The man dumped food into the first bowl. Most of the puppies pushed and shoved to get a spot to eat. Some of the more aggressive puppies, growled and bit anyone who got in their way.

Lav and Kama had learned that it was better to wait for one of the last bowls to be filled. They got just as much food without the hassle of a crowd.

At least, that's usually how feedings worked. After emptying food into the first two bowls, the man's phone rang.

"Hello...How big of a mess?"

"Come on, just pour us some food," Kama said.

The man set the food down. The handle clanked against the side of the bucket. He pulled a mop from his cart and left the room. Kama and Lav barked, hoping he would come back. Then they waited and waited. Finally, the other puppies finished the food in the bowls and barked too. When the man did return, he gave the dogs the rest of the food, but there was only enough left to fill the same two bowls he had filled earlier.

All the puppies tried to squeeze around the bowls. This time, Lav struggled to get a spot too. He swallowed each mouthful quickly, so he could take another bite before it was gone.

Pain shot through his leg. "Ouch," Lav yelped.

"Out of the way," Cryp said, "or I'll bite you even harder."

"Knock it off. I've hardly eaten anything," Lav barked. "Besides, you already had a lot."

Wrinkles formed on Cryp's nose as he flashed his teeth and growled.

"Lav, give him your spot," Kama said.

She was the only puppy that bothered to lift her head from the bowls. The rest were too busy eating the dwindling supply of food.

"But, I was here first," Lav whined.

Cryp lunged forward. This time he sank his teeth deep into Lav's front leg.

Lav shrieked. The sound finally caught the attention of the man cleaning the pen.

The man rushed over. "That's enough you two."

Lav limped away from the other puppies. Blood matted the fur on his front leg, which throbbed every time he put too much weight on that paw. He didn't focus on the pain for long though. The man not only picked Lav up, but cradled him in his arms before stepping outside the pen.

Lav was thrilled to finally leave the pen, but that changed as the man carried him out of the puppy room. Florescent lights brightened the ceiling panels. The floor and walls of the hallway were unnaturally white. Lav's body grew tense as he realized the world is a lot bigger than he ever imagined.

Chapter 3

The man walked down the hallway. New smells tickled Lav's nostrils. The strongest odors were from chemicals the humans used to keep the laboratory clean. The rest of the odors were musty, the way soggy paper on the floor of the puppy pen smells by the end of the day.

The man eventually carried him into another room. A sign above the door read, "Mini Room." Against one side of the Mini Room was a long countertop, covered with cages. The opposite wall had fish tanks, stacked three aquariums high.

Two humans were there, the ones that stuck him with needles. The first, a woman, with light brown hair pulled back into a ponytail; the other, a bald man with dark skin.

"They're mini alright, but wild as ever," the bald human said. "Too wild to be pets."

The woman poked a measuring stick into the cage. "Maybe there's a way to tame them down a notch or two. I'll run few scenarios through the computer model."

The humans jumped backward as something inside hit the measuring stick and snarled.

"Dr. Bray, there was a bit of an accident," the man holding Lav said. "A couple pups got into a fight."

"Let's take a look," the bald human replied. He put some rubber gloves on and leaned over Lav, reaching out to touch the injured leg.

Lav growled. Dr. Bray didn't stop. Lav tried to jump to the floor, but the man holding him tightened his grip. Lav squirmed and yelped. The only human he had ever trusted was trapping him.

Dr. Bray touched Lav's leg and bent his ankle back and forth. A jolt of pain shot through his body. Lav shrieked.

"He's alright," Dr. Bray said, "but he'll limp for a few days."

The woman leaned over, peering into another cage. "Jim, don't let this happen again. Those dogs are a lot harder to replace than you are."

"Yes, ma'am, it won't," the man holding Lav said.

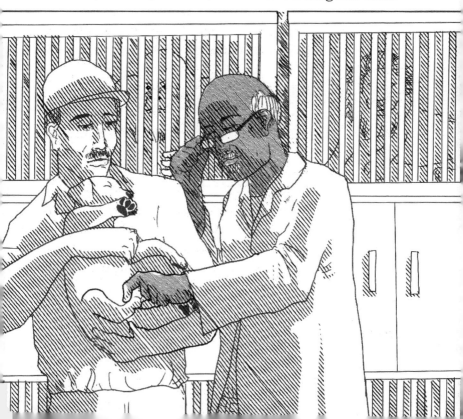

Lav glanced at the cages on the counter. They contained animals he had never seen before.

"Hey, what are you staring at," one creature said. "What? Haven't you seen a mini lion before?"

The creature looked like an adult lion, but was about the same size as Lav. The Lion paced back and forth in his cage.

"Relax Daniel," a gorilla in the cage next to him said. The gorilla sat near the front of the cage and was as small as the lion. "He's just a puppy. You know he's never seen miniatures before."

"You're lucky these bars are between the two of us. Otherwise, I'd make sure you were limping on your other three legs too," Daniel said.

The gorilla shook his head. "Don't mind him. He acts like this with everyone."

Chapter 4

Lav was relieved when Jim finished talking. He carried Lav back to the puppy room and set him in the pen. A few minutes later, Jim carried cages into the room, fourteen cages to be exact. He stacked them one on top of the other, until there were two rows of seven. Then Jim began to put a puppy in each one.

Lav noticed that Jim left the pen's door open just a crack as he carried two more puppies to the cages. His hands were too full to close it all the way.

"Let's go," Lav said. He limped toward the open door.

"What are you doing?" Kama asked.

"He's going to lock us in cages, like the animals I saw in the other room. We have to go *now*." Lav glanced at Jim to make sure he wasn't watching. "We can find someplace else to live," he said.

Kama tilted her head. "Where would we live?"

"I don't know," Lav admitted. "The hallway...or maybe outside, where the humans take you."

"You can't live out there," Cryp said, as Jim returned to the pen and picked up two more puppies. "How will you eat if you don't have humans to give you food?"

"I don't know. I'll worry about that later," Lav said. "Come on, we have to go."

Kama's tail wagged. She ran in front of Lav and used her paw to pull the pen's door open. She waited for Lav to get out before dashing into the hallway.

Lav hobbled as fast as he could. Just as he was leaving the room, he heard barking.

"Hey, human! Human," Cryp shouted at Jim, who was setting another puppy into a cage. "They're getting away. Over there."

Jim looked around the pen to see what was wrong. He spotted Lav and Kama. "Oh no you don't," he said, and rushed after them.

Kama's tail no longer wagged. "Hurry Lav."

Lav quickened his pace, but his leg throbbed with pain. It felt like it would take him hours to make it down the long hallway.

"I can't. Just go."

Kama sprinted ahead but stopped when the woman Lav had seen earlier walked out of a room in front of her. Kama turned around, but Jim blocked her retreat.

"Lav," Kama whimpered. She crouched low to the floor. Her body shook. "We're trapped."

"Is there a problem?" the woman asked. She bent over, scooped Kama into her arms, and handed her to Jim.

"No ma'am. I was just putting the puppies into cages." Jim carried Kama back toward the puppy room. "I'll be back for you," he muttered to Lav, as he passed by.

Lav would have made one more desperate attempt to get away, if it weren't for the woman standing there. She crossed her arms, held her lips tight together, and waited.

Dr. Bray poked his head out of a room and called down the hallway. "Shannon, I want to know what you think of this."

"Just a moment," the woman said. Shannon glared at Lav with her intense, dark eyes. Finally, Jim returned.

"Thank you," Jim said. He picked Lav off the floor and carried him to an empty cage.

Lav barked at Jim as he locked the metal door. First, Jim would not let him go and let the bald man touch his leg. Now, Jim was putting him in a cage, with hardly any room to play.

"I hate humans!" Lav shouted. "I hate them, hate them, hate them."

"It's alright," Jim said, after hearing the tone of Lav's bark. "Now you don't have to worry about fighting. You'll be safe in there."

Chapter 5

Lav spun in circles. He nibbled on the cage bars. He jumped up and down, over and over again. He even barked at the fire alarm above the doorway, because it had a little red light that blinked on and off. He did just about anything he could think of to have fun inside of his cage. The problem was he wasn't having fun. These were the only things he could do to keep from going crazy with boredom.

The other puppies were already used to their tiny cages. Even when they lived in the pen, they had slept most of the day. They didn't care whether they had a lot of room to sleep or not.

Kama was still the only puppy that would play with Lav. Since Jim cleaned their cages every day and never seemed to remember which cage belonged to which puppy, they were always given a new neighbor. Some days, Lav and Kama were put right next to each other. Then, they would race from the front of their cage to the back, jump against the wall that they shared, and stick their paws into each other's cages.

The problem was all the other days. When they weren't close to each other, Kama stopped playing. She would lay in a corner for hours with her head resting on the floor. Sometimes, she fell asleep, but usually she just laid there.

Kama's energy seemed to be disappearing. She began to act like the rest of the puppies. Lav felt like he was losing his only friend.

It was just another boring day, when Kama lifted her head. Her ears turned forward.

"Someone's coming," she said. Kama stood up and poked her nose through the cage bars. Her nostrils flared with each sniff. "It's the people in white coats, but...," Kama listened. "There's another human with them. I don't recognize his voice."

Soon, Lav could hear them too. When the humans entered the room, their muffled voices became a loud conversation.

The other puppies woke up and barked. Once they saw that the people did not bring food, they laid back down.

"Right over here Lieutenant," Dr. Bray said.

Beside him stood Shannon and a man Lav did not recognize. Shannon and Dr. Bray wore white lab coats, like normal. The third person wore light green clothes with dark patches on the shoulders. He walked to Cryp's cage and peered inside. Then he moved to Kama's, always keeping his back abnormally strait.

"They were designed to be hunting dogs," Shannon said, "but I think you'll find their abilities to be useful for the military too."

Kama backed away from the human. Her tail pulled between her legs and she pressed her body against the far corner of the cage.

"We've enhanced their sense of smell with DNA from rats and bears," Dr. Bray said. "Cat traits and a few owl genes have helped with their hearing too."

"Cats," the man in green repeated.

Dr. Bray nodded. "Cats can hear a wider range of frequencies."

"But it's their sense of smell that we've improved the most," Shannon said, "and their camouflaged fur is an extra bonus."

"Lav, why are they looking at me?" Kama asked.

The stiff looking man leaned close to Kama's cage and peered inside. "Hi girl. It's O.K. I just want to see what you can do."

At first Lav was scared, but then the man poked a finger into Kama's cage and whistled. Lav ran forward. "Hey! Leave her alone," he barked.

The man opened the door to her cage and reached in.

"Help!" Kama screamed.

Chapter 6

Lav jumped against the front of his cage. He barked as viciously as he could. "Let go of her," he shouted, as the man picked Kama up and held her in his arms.

Kama's whole body shook. "Put me down! I don't know you!"

Dr. Bray opened Cryp's cage and took him out too.

"Shall we," Shannon said, leading the others to the hallway.

"What are you going to do to us," Kama whined.

"Run away," Lav shouted.

Kama tried to wiggle out of the man's arms, but couldn't. "Help," she cried, one last time.

"Kama! Bring her back!" Lav barked. He threw himself against the front of his cage over and over again.

"That dog has completely lost it," one of the other puppies said.

"He's going to hurt himself," said another.

Lav didn't care though. He didn't trust humans, not the ones in white coats, and especially not the human with shoulder patches.

What if they hurt her, he thought. *What if they never bring her back?*

Lav was so angry he didn't notice his cage sliding forward each time he lunged at the bars. Eventually, his cage slipped off the one underneath. It crashed against the floor, forcing the door to pop open.

Lav slowly sat up. His head ached. He could smell the blood seeping beneath the fur on his forehead. Realizing that he was free, Lav stepped out of the cage and ran into the hallway.

Lav could hardly smell Kama's scent and had no idea which direction she had gone. The only place he recognized was the room Jim had carried him into, the Mini Room.

He trotted down the hall and peeked around the doorframe. No humans were there.

"Hey, look who we have here," Daniel said.

The gorilla was hunched over his food bowl, eating a thin slice of banana. He straightened his back when he noticed Lav. "How did you get out?" the gorilla asked, rushing to the front of his cage.

Lav stepped further into the room. "Did the humans come here with two puppies? One is named Kama. I think they're taking her outside."

"They walked past the door a few minutes ago," the gorilla replied.

"Which way did they go?" Lav asked.

"Let us out, and we'll show you," the gorilla said. "We'll go outside with you."

Lav hesitated. He didn't trust the creature.

"How can we help if we're locked up?" the gorilla asked.

"Yea, let us out," Daniel said.

Lav turned to the lion. "Why should I let you out? Last time I was here, you wanted to hurt me."

"Don't worry about him," the gorilla interrupted. "Besides, you always seem to be hurt anyway."

Lav lifted his front paw and wiped some of the blood off his forehead. He could hear humans talking in the hallway.

"Dog, listen to me." the gorilla said quietly. "Soon the humans will see you and try to catch you. You'll need all the help you can get."

Lav stared at the gorilla. "Alright," he finally said, stand back. I'm gonna knock your cage down. That's how mine opened."

The gorilla crawled to the back of his cage and gripped the bars.

Lav jumped off the ground and tried to grab the cage with his teeth. They just slipped across the front of the bars. Lav fell back to the ground.

"Try again dog." the gorilla said.

Lav tried many times. Eventually, his teeth caught the bars enough to pull the cage forward. A few tries later, he pushed the cage further onto the counter by accident. Finally, his teeth locked onto one of the corners. As Lav fell back down, the cage was yanked off the counter. It smashed to the ground, but the door didn't open.

"What was that," a human's voice said from the hallway.

"Congo? Are you O.K.," Daniel whispered.

"I'm fine," the gorilla said. He climbed to the front of his cage, which was now the ceiling, and grabbed the door. He shook the door as hard as he could. The whole cage rattled.

Daniel glared at Lav. "You're a lousy liar," he growled.

"No, it worked for my cage," Lav insisted. "I swear. That's how my door opened."

Congo stopped shaking his cage, then stared at the doorway. "Hide. Someone's coming. Go! Quick!"

Lav rushed to the far side of the room. He crouched beside an aquarium just as Jim appeared in the doorway.

"What's going on in here?" Jim asked.

"Pssst."

Lav looked into the aquarium. A miniature whale swam closer. A second whale rose to the surface. "Pssst" was the only sound the whale made as it blew air from its body. The air made water droplets spray from its back, but the droplets were not much larger than the fizz that rises from a can of soda.

Jim walked to Congo. "How did you get down there?" he asked. Jim lifted the cage and set it back on the counter. After peering at the gorilla to make sure it was alright, Jim left the room.

Lav crept away from the aquarium. "I'm sorry, but I have to go. I need to find my friend."

Congo's head bowed, as if he were heartbroken. "I understand dog. Thanks for trying."

"Thanks for trying? How about thanks for nothing," Daniel said. "You could have killed him."

Lav ran to the door. He peeked into the hallway. Jim was still walking away from the Mini Room. When Jim rounded a corner, Lav ran in the other direction.

"Wrong way," Congo shouted. "Good luck," he added, as Lav trotted past the Mini Room's door, in the same direction Jim had gone.

Chapter 7

Kama and Cryp were carried outside. Shannon squirted a piece of cloth with a spray bottle, and held the cloth out for Cryp to smell.

"This is TNT powder mixed with water," she explained. "Your average bomb sniffing dog can detect the scent when the solution is diluted at a one to three thousand ratio." She could no longer hold back a smile. "This solution is a one-to-ten-thousand ratio."

Cryp was set down after he finished smelling the cloth. He kept his nose close to the ground and slowly wandered away. When he found the scent trail, he followed it at a faster pace. It led him to a dozen overturned buckets. He sniffed them one at a time, until he knew which bucket had the strongest odor. Then he sat down next to it.

Shannon, who had been following Cryp, kicked the bucket over. Underneath was another piece of cloth.

"Good boy," she said.

The Lieutenant raised his eyebrows. "Very impressive," he said, while petting the fur on Kama's back. "Can she smell as good as that one?"

"Yes, but we've been training her differently," Shannon explained. "As you saw, Cryp has been taught to detect a variety of explosive chemicals. Kama on the other hand, is being trained as a search dog. We wanted to prove that our canines can be used for many different purposes."

"How many more like this do you have?"

"Right now, just these two," Shannon said, "but if you give us enough time and money, the army can have more, a lot more."

The Lieutenant nodded. "I'm going to assign two of my top dog handlers to this facility. Give them the freedom to change the training schedules however they see fit."

"No problem," Shannon said.

"Good. They'll be here tomorrow morning."

Chapter 8

Lav looked in every room he passed. The Kitten, Rabbit, Hamster, Bird, Venomless, Mega, Glow, and Plant rooms didn't have Kama or any humans in them. When he reached the end of one hall, he walked down another. Finally, he found a sent he recognized. It wasn't Kama's scent, but food.

He trotted across the tiled floor and found the room the food smell was coming from. Inside, there were dozens of cardboard boxes. A machine filled the room with a continuous, rumbling noise.

Lav walked in and sniffed the boxes. They each seemed to be full of food. Some he recognized as the food the puppies were given and others seemed to be filled with foods he had never tried before. He ran from box to box, curious to smell what was in each one. The room seemed like the perfect place for him and Kama to live. No cages and plenty to eat.

"That's all of it," a human's voice said.

Jim entered the room with a woman. She wore a brown uniform. Lav would have heard them coming sooner, but the loud noise had muffled their voices.

Lav ran to the far side of the room, through a giant doorway, and into what seemed to be a smaller, darker room. Inside, more boxes were stacked to the ceiling. The noise was a lot louder in there too. Lav darted behind one of the boxes. He wiggled as close to the cardboard as he could and flattened his body against the floor, which was cold and vibrated with the noise.

The humans walked up to the giant doorway.

"So, what are you guys hiding here anyways?" the woman asked, as she swung one large door closed.

The room grew darker.

"What makes you think we have something to hide?" Jim asked.

"Every time I make a delivery here, someone escorts me through the building."

Jim paused as if he was going to lie but knew she wouldn't believe him. "Hopefully, in a few years we can tell people. For now, it's top secret though."

"Fair enough," the woman said, and slammed the second door shut.

The room became completely dark. A while later, the constant noise grew louder. Lav felt the floor move more than before too. His body rocked back and forth. His side bumped into the box. Lav didn't like the darkness. He didn't like the moving floor. He wanted to leave the room. He had to leave the room. Lav yelped and barked for help, but the doors did not open.

The delivery truck left the laboratory, which was a small building compared to the ones under construction nearby. Fenced in cows, sheep, and other animals watched the truck drive away. It sped along a road that wound through experimental gardens, fields, and orchards. Finally, the truck passed under an archway and entered the mountain forest that surrounded the valley.

Chapter 9

Dr. Bray pointed at the empty cage lying on the floor. "Look at that," he said, as they were returning Kama and Cryp to the Puppy Room.

Shannon locked Kama in her cage and dashed into the hallway. "One of the puppies is out," she shouted. "Start searching rooms!"

"Where's Lav?" Kama asked when she realized what the commotion was about.

The other puppies had moved to the front of their cages to see why the humans were yelling. Their tails wagged due to the rare excitement.

"I think he ran away," Violetta said.

"What do you mean, ran away?"

"He starting acting nuts, then knocked his cage over and left. He didn't come back after that.

Kama sat down. "Lav wouldn't do that. He wouldn't leave, not without telling me. I bet he'll be back any minute."

Kama listen for his footsteps. She sniffed the air, hoping he was still nearby. Only old scent remained.

Kama heard something. People were coming to the puppy room. They were coming faster than normal. She backed further into her cage.

"Let's really test these puppies out," Dr. Bray said. He rushed into the room and went straight for Cryp's cage. Shannon was not far behind and swung Kama's door open.

"What now?" Kama asked.

"I don't know. I thought we were done," Cryp replied.

To their amazement, the humans set them on the floor near Lav's cage. Shannon pushed Kama forward, forcing her head inside.

"Get a good sniff," Shannon said. "This is important."

Dr. Bray pulled a cloth out of his pocket and wiped all around the bottom of Lav's cage. "Here, let's try this." he said, and held the cloth out for Kama and Cryp to smell.

"They want us to find Lav," Kama said.

"Is that what they're freaking out about?" Cryp asked. "We already know his scent." Cryp put his nose to the ground and followed Lav's scent trail.

"Thata boy," Dr. Bray said.

Kama sniffed too, following the same path as Cryp out of the room.

Chapter 10

In the darkness, Lav lost all sense of time. The cold floor made him shiver. The chilly air seeped through his fur. Everything shook, rocked, and bounced. He felt sick. Just when it seemed like he would be trapped forever, the shaking stopped. The loud noise softened. A minute later, one of the giant doors opened. The brightest light Lav had ever seen flooded into the room. He squeezed his eyes shut.

Thump. Thump. Thump.

Lav peaked around the box. The woman in brown uniform had climbed into the room and was walking closer. Lav wanted to run, but his body felt stiff. He waited for the woman to pick him up. Instead, she bent down, lifted a nearby box, and walked out the giant doors.

Lav sat up and waited. He crept toward the giant doors. Countless new scents overwhelmed his nose. For the first time, he saw the sky. He saw grass and trees too. There was even a bee flying from one dandelion to the next.

Lav peered outside. The delivery woman was knocking on the front of a house. He leaped to the ground and was startled by the way dirt felt beneath his feet. Lav looked for a new place to hide. A large building was not far away. He ran.

The building reminded Lav of the laboratory. There were hundreds of animals inside, everything was white, and smelled sterilized.

Although Lav wasn't eager to go back inside of a building, he was happy to be someplace that felt familiar. Anywhere outside the moving
room and away from humans seemed like a good place to be.

The closer Lav trotted to the animals the more he realized just how large they were. He sat and watched. They took turns walking into cages just large enough to fit a single creature. A machine slowly moved their cages so an empty cage would appear for the next creature to walk into.

"Look at that," a cow said, and began to laugh.

Lav stood, realizing the cow was laughing at him.

"What happened to you?" a different cow asked.

"Looks like he ate a few too many grapes," said another.

"Naw, that's just what happens when they roll around in manure too long."

"What do you mean?" Lav asked.

"Your fur," a cow began, but could hardly stop chuckling. "It's purple."

After realizing that these creatures must not be that smart, Lav decided to look for a place to hide. The problem was, wherever he went in the building, there were cows there to laugh at him. Soon, he found himself in the center of the machine that was slowly making the creatures' cages move. Their cages spun in a circle around him and they were teasing him from all different directions.

"Is that what happens to animals when they eat too much people food?"

"No, that's what anyone looks like after whiffing one of Buttercup's farts."

The cows stomped their feet, threw their heads into the air, and laughed.

"What's your guys' problem?" Lav barked. "Haven't you seen a purple dog before?"

This just made them laugh even louder.

"Come on dog, stop it. My udders are full," a cow giggled, then stopped to catch its breath. "It hurts too much to laugh."

"Seriously dog, what happened to you? Did you fall in paint or something?"

"No."

"Lick your fur! Prove it," another bellowed.

Lav licked the fur on the front of his leg.

"Holy human!" one shouted. "It's dried on already."

"What a freak," another said. "There's something seriously wrong with you."

Lav looked at his fur, then back at the cows. Starting to feel hurt by their comments he hurried out of the building.

Chapter 11

Kama and Cryp led the humans to the door of the Mini Room. They didn't go in. It was clear that Lav's scent also led right back out. They continued down the hallway and into the truck loading station.

"That food sure smells good," Cryp said, referring to all the boxes in the room.

Kama sniffed the floor, and then sniffed the boxes. "He must have walked all over the room," she said. "It's like he was smelling every single box. I can't tell which trail is the freshest."

Cryp and Kama wandered from box to box trying to figure out where Lav had last walked. At one point, Kama followed his trail to where the delivery truck had been parked, but since the large garage door was closed, she thought it was a wall and that her nose was mistaken.

"Stupid dogs," Shannon said. "They just smell food. There's nothing here."

Shannon and Dr. Bray picked up the puppies and brought them back to their cages.

Chapter 12

Lav ran across the countryside the rest of the day. All the other animals stared and snickered at him, just like the cows had. He found red chickens with yellow chicks. He saw green-headed ducks, blue jays, orange cats, and pink pigs. No other animal was purple, which made Lav wonder if these animals were right. Maybe he was a freak.

The outside world was a harsh place. Lav wanted to return to the Puppy Room and would have gladly gone back into his cage, but he didn't know where the Puppy Room was. He was lost.

Lav slowly walked into a barn as the first stars appeared for the night. There were other animals there too. They whispered to one another.

"Who is that?"

"What is that?"

"I've never seen a dog that color before."

"You sure it's a dog?"

Lav cried. The whispering and everything else that had happened was too much to bear. The hay he walked across reminded him of the paper shreds that had covered the floor of the puppy pen. It was the only comfort he had experienced all day.

Lav stuck out his tongue and yawned. He was tired of the laughing, tired from running, tired from the small room he had been trapped in, tired of worrying about Kama, and tired of not knowing where he was. Lav snuggled into the hay, curled his body, and cried himself to sleep.

Chapter 13

"They're still looking for him," Congo said, as humans searched the Mini Room a ninth time.

Daniel continued to lay on his side. He didn't bother to lift his head. "Just go to sleep already."

"You don't get it," Congo said. "If they're still looking, it means the purple dog got away."

"Yea and we're still here," Daniel groaned.

Congo grasped the bars on his cage. "But if he got away, that means it really is possible."

"What's possible?" Daniel asked.

"It means there's a way out of here."

Shannon was on her hands and knees in the Mini Room. She was looking under every chair and table, when Dr. Bray came in.

"We checked the surveillance tapes," he said.

"And?"

"The hunting pups were right. The last footage we have of him was going into the loading station."

"Then why wasn't he there," Shannon ask.

"Don't know. We did receive a delivery around that time, but nobody saw him. We even called the truck driver, asked if she saw anything unusual during her route. She said, 'It was a normal day.'"

Shannon rubbed her forehead with her fingertips. "If anyone sees that dog, our secret is blown. We're not ready for that yet. Not even close."

Chapter 14

Johnny followed his grandma into the barn. A basket swung by his side. "When I grow up I'm going to be a farmer," he said. "and live here with you."

"You wouldn't want to be a farmer here," his grandmother replied.

"Why? You have a barn and animals."

"Yea, but this is just a hobby farm."

"What do you mean?" Johnny asked.

"There's only one cow in the barn and I don't even milk her."

"But we could get more cows in here."

"Only forty or so," the woman said, as they came to the chicken nests.

She stopped to look around the barn and remembered many years past. "There was a time when your grandpa and I made a living on this place, but that time is long gone. Farming is different now."

"Why is it different?" Johnny asked, as he checked for eggs.

"It might be hard for you to understand but you're growing up in a very different world than the one I've lived in," the woman said.

She watched the boy put an egg into the basket. "To make it as a farmer these days, you need to have huge herds of cattle or massive fields to plant, and then you need fancy machines to help you do the work. Farming is just different."

"So this farm is too small to be a farm anymore," Johnny asked.

"I'm afraid so," the woman said. She watched the boy pick up a second egg, but instead of putting it in the basket he rotated it in his fingers a while. "But yes, you may live here when you grow up," she added. "That is, if you'll still want to."

"I'll want to," Johnny said, without hesitation. He finally put the second egg into the basket.

The grandmother smiled. "For the time being though, the animals and I are sure glad that you are able to visit on the weekends like you do."

Johnny tried to peer under a hen that was on its nest. "I don't like how things change." he said.

"Are you still talking about farming, or your mother's contract in Ecuador?" the grandmother asked.

"Both," he admitted.

"Change is scary. Isn't it?"

Johnny didn't answer.

"Sometimes, it feels like the world is changing faster and faster," the grandmother said. "It used to scare me too, but I've found that it's impossible to keep things as they are. Our time is best spent making sure that when things do change, they change for the better."

Chapter 15

Lav realized he was not dreaming. The human scent he smelled was real, and close by. Lav quickly sat up. As he did, the straw beneath him rustled.

"Oh my!"

Lav jumped at the sound of the woman's voice. She was near the chickens and not alone. Beside her was the smallest human Lav had ever seen.

"Well aren't you cute," the woman said. She forced her stiff body to lean over. Her hair was gray and wavy. She lowered a wrinkled hand close to the ground for Lav to smell, but he backed away.

The little human set down his basket. He crouched and also wanted his hand to be smelled.

The woman stood again. "Shy, aren't you?"

Johnny glanced at his grandma. "Is that a dog?"

"Sure looks like it," she said. "You stay and watch. I'll get some food." She picked up the egg basket and hurried out of the barn.

Lav listened. The screen door on the farmhouse slammed shut. He wanted to run but Johnny was between him and the door. He didn't dare go closer.

The screen door slammed again. The grandmother walked back into the barn. She carried a bowl in one hand and a plate that had leftover chicken roast in the other. She laid the bowl on the ground and set a small piece of chicken in the middle of it.

Lav tilted his head to the side. He looked at the chicken. Then, he looked at the humans.

"Have it your way," the woman said. She took a couple steps away from the bowl and motioned for Johnny to do the same.

Lav slowly walked closer. He hadn't eaten since breaking out of his cage. With each step, the wonderful smell of food grew stronger. He gobbled the piece of meat as soon as he reached the bowl. He backed away when he was finished.

The humans came forward again and set more meat in the bowl. Although they backed away from the food again, they stayed a little closer. This process was repeated many times until the humans practically stood next to the bowl and dropped new pieces of meat into it. Finally, when the woman was setting yet another chunk of meat down, Johnny crouched to pet the puppy.

Lav instinctively bit the little hand, like he had done to the humans in white coats so many times.

The woman shrieked and Johnny pulled his hand away. "Are you alright?" she asked.

Johnny rubbed his hand. "There's no blood," he said, but his arm remained close to his body.

"I know. We shouldn't have tricked you," the grandmother said. Lav backed away as the woman dumped the remaining chicken into the bowl. "Go ahead and eat," she said. "We'll leave you be."

The woman turned around and put an arm around Johnny. The humans left the barn. This time, the screen door only slammed once as they entered the farmhouse and Lav continued to eat.

Chapter 16

A cat leapt down from a dusty tractor tire. "Biting the hand that feeds you, what gratitude."

"The little human tried to touch me," Lav said.

"Oh no! He's going to pet me to death," the cat teased. It walked to the bowl and started eating too. "My name's Lexie. What's yours?"

"Lav," he said, between bites.

"You sure cried a lot last night Lav. If your fur wasn't so purple, I would think you were blue."

"Ha, hilarious. Are you just going to tease me too?"

"Give me a break," Lexie said. "I'm just trying to talk."

"Don't take it personally," a tall animal in one of the barn stalls said. "Nobody on the farm had seen a llama before I came here. At first, they wouldn't stop calling me 'Goose Neck,' but then they got to know me."

"Yea, it also helps that your real name is 'Spit-Shot,'" Lexie said. She gave Lav a wink. "Trust me, it's a bad idea to make fun of an animal with a name like that."

"How come?" Lav asked.

"Do you see that bucket?" Spit-Shot asked.

"Yea."

Something shot out of the llama's mouth. It was a glob of spit that not only landed in the bucket but had enough force to knock it over.

"That's disgusting," Lav said.

Lexie shuddered at the sight of the spit. "So Lav, let's start over," she said. "I've never met anyone like you before. Where are you from?"

Since Lav was lost, he couldn't really tell the animals where he came from. He described the Puppy Room, the hallway, and the Mini Room the best he could. Then, he explained how he became lost while looking for Kama. As he told his story, the other animals listened and sometimes asked questions about his strange home.

"Well, I want to apologize for how those cows treated you," Daisy said. She was the last milk cow living on the farm, and stood in a stall neighboring Spit-Shot's. "What a bunch of disrespectful cattle."

"Thanks Daisy," Lav said.

"Those humans too," Spit-Shot added, "the green one and ones in white jackets sound awful."

"Yea, you should stay here and serve these humans," Lexie said.

"Why would I serve the humans?"

"That's what we're supposed to do," Lexie said.

Lav tilted his head to the side, "Says who?"

"The creator," Lexie said. "He gave every animal a job. Ours is to serve humans."

"Cows give the humans milk," Daisy explained, "and the hens give the humans eggs."

"And dogs and cats are companions for the humans," Lexie added. "We give them friendship."

"But why should animals do all of these things for humans?" Lav asked.

"Because the humans were given a job too," Daisy said. "The most important one. They were made to care for all plants and animals."

"Well, they do a lousy job," Lav said.

"Not all humans are good at their job, but some animals aren't good at their job either," Daisy said.

"Like a dog that bites humans for no reason," Lexie pointed out.

Chapter 17

"Are you sure you want to go through with this?" Dr. Bray asked. "Modifying animals is one thing, but human modifications...you could be thrown into prison."

Shannon stuffed a laptop and some papers into her brief case. For once, she wasn't wearing a lab coat over her business casual clothes. "Not if I do it in Greece or dozens of other open-minded countries," she said, "It's only illegal here."

Dr. Bray rubbed the back of his bald head. "I know, but with everything going on: Lav missing and the army monitoring us."

"I agree, it's not the ideal time for me to be away, but I won't push this back. I've been planning too long," Shannon said. "Just make sure to update me at least twice a day. I'll probably be calling more times than that anyway."

Dr. Bray nodded.

Shannon took a deep breath and looked around her office one last time. "Alright, I'll be back in about nine months."

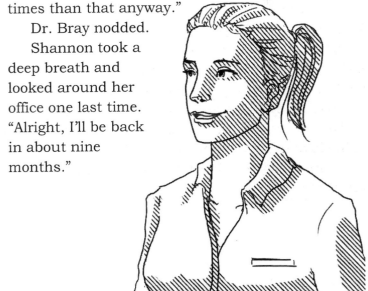

Chapter 18

Lav jumped when he heard the screen door slam again. The sound of running feet was getting closer. Johnny darted into the barn. The old woman was not far behind.

"Good, you're still here," the boy said, when he saw Lav. "We brought you more food. You want some?"

Johnny scrapped leftover spaghetti into the bowl and backed away as he had before.

"You don't need to be afraid," Lexie said. She walked to the bowl and started eating. "These humans are nice."

"Why is this human so small?" Lav asked.

"He's a child," Daisy said.

"A child," Lav repeated.

"A young dog is a puppy. A young human is a child," Daisy explained.

"And most children are harmless," Lexie added. She ran to the boy's feet and purred. She leaned against him and let her fur glide against the side of his leg.

Johnny bent over and slid his hand along Lexie's back.

"Look out," Lav barked.

"Relax, will you. He's just petting me."

Lav watched Lexie roll onto her back, so the boy could scratch her stomach too. "It feels great," she said. "Come over here."

Lav thought about it and decided to trust the cat. He took a few cautious steps toward the human, and then stopped.

When Johnny saw the puppy moving closer, he held his hand out so it could be smelled. "It's alright. Come here puppy. Here Purple Pup."

"That's a good name for him," the grandmother said.

"What's he doing now?" Lav asked, when the boy began to whistle and make clicking sounds with his tongue.

"I don't know," Lexie said. "For some reason, humans do that when they want you to come closer to them."

"It's alright Lav. Go on," Spit-Shot said. "I've got you covered. If he tries anything funny, I'll spit at him. I promise."

"He's not going to do anything," Lexie said. "Now, get over here."

Lav crept toward Johnny and smelt his fingers. Johnny slowly moved closer and lowered his hand to Lav's back. Lav crouched lower and lower so that the hand would not touch him. When his body was against the ground he could not move any lower. The hand touched his fur. The boy was petting him.

"See, I told you it feels good," Lexie said.

Lav had to wait a while to decide what he thought of this new feeling. "It's not bad," he admitted.

The woman came closer and petted Lav too. "Why, I've never felt such soft fur," she said. "You really are something special. Aren't you?"

Lav could tell her words were kind. He could sense their love. His tail began to sway back and forth.

It swung so hard that it sometimes slapped against the side of his body, and it didn't stop wagging the rest of the afternoon.

Chapter 19

"Hey girl, I'm Dana, your new trainer," a woman said, "We'll be doing things a little different today."

"These people are weird," Kama said, as Dana held a shoe in front of Kama's nose. "Mine just has human scent on it."

A young man held a cloth out for Cryp to smell.

"Mine smells the same," Cryp said, referring to the familiar odor of C4.

"Maybe they lost someone," Kama said. "I think they want me to help find them."

Kama sniffed the ground and soon found a trail where the human had been walking. Since there was a leash around her neck, she could only follow the trail as fast as her trainer could jog.

She led her trainer across a mud puddle, up some stairs, but stopped at the narrow board that went from the top of the stairs to another platform.

"Keep going, girl," Dana said. "You can do it."

Kama carefully stepped onto the board and walked to the other side. She hopped off the platform and followed the scent trail to a garbage bin. She sniffed the bin. The human she was looking for was definitely in there.

Kama sat and barked.

"Good girl," Dana said, and held out a dog treat. "Come out," Dana yelled. "She found you."

A moment later, the lid to the garbage can lifted and a man climbed out.

Chapter 20

"You're supposed to let go," Johnny said, as he tried to pull a tennis ball out of Lav's mouth.

Lav shook his head, playfully trying to keep the ball for himself.

The farmhouse door slammed shut.

"He'll fetch, but won't give it back," Johnny hollered to his grandmother, as she walked down the steps.

"You'll have to finish teaching him next weekend," she called back. "Your mother just called. She's almost here."

Johnny stopped tugging on the ball and ran to the house to get his things. Lav pounced beside him, but stopped as the boy ran up the steps and into the house. Lav realized that children are not only small, like puppies are, but they enjoy playing as much as puppies do too. Although Lav was no longer afraid of the grandmother, he enjoyed spending most of his time with Johnny.

Johnny rushed outside as a car pulled into the farmyard. He set the luggage bag he carried on the ground and picked Lav up.

"Look Mom," he shouted. "You have to feel his fur."

A woman wearing a gray business suit stepped out of the car. "What did you do to that poor thing?"

"I didn't do anything. He's just purple. We named him Purple Pup. He had blood on his head when we found him, but Grandma helped me clean it off."

Johnny's mother came and scratched behind Lav's ears. It seemed that all of the humans around the farm were nice to him. Lav could hardly believe that he had hated humans just a day ago.

After giving Lav a gentle hug, Johnny said, "Goodbye."

"What's he doing?" Lav asked, as Johnny climbed into his mother's car.

"I told you he doesn't always live here like the old woman. He just stays at the farm every once in a while," Lexie said. "Don't worry. He'll come back again."

Johnny rolled down the car window and shouted to Lav, "Be good for grandma boy, and don't chase the chickens."

There was something in Johnny's voice that let Lav know that the boy loved him. He could feel it in his heart.

Lav had a doggy grin on his face as the car backed out of the driveway. For the first time in his life, Lav felt like he had a home; like he belonged somewhere. The only thing that was missing was Kama. She would like playing in the huge yard. Lav knew she would love the boy too. The three of them playing together was the only thing Lav could think of that would have turned this great day into a perfect one.

Part 2
The Return

Chapter 21

Johnny and Lav ran across the yard. Eventually, Johnny's grandma walked down the porch steps but continued to hold onto the railing.

Johnny picked up a tattered tennis ball from the grass. When Lav caught glimpse of it he barked and leaped into the air.

"Go get it boy," Johnny shouted.

Lav dashed after the ball. He caught it in his jaws while it was still rolling. Lav was full grown, fast, and strong. He had been on the farm so long now he seemed to fit right in with the rest of the animals. It was hard for him to remember living anywhere else. Kama and the Puppy Room almost felt like a dream. His purple fur was the only proof that they weren't just dreams, but memories.

Lav rushed back to Johnny and dropped the ball by his feet.

"Good job," Johnny said, and scratched behind Lav's ears.

Growing impatient, Lav nudged the ball closer to Johnny.

"Alright. One more time," Johnny said, and threw the ball again.

Lav didn't chase after it. He ran to the old woman who was bending forward. She leaned one hand on her knee. The other still held onto the railing for balance. By the time Lav reached her, the woman had lowered herself to the ground.

"Grandma," Johnny shouted, and soon he was kneeling in the grass beside her. He pulled a cell phone out of his pocket and dialed 9-1-1. He stayed on the phone with the dispatcher until the ambulance arrived. After that he called his father.

Lexie came into the yard and sat next to Lav. The old woman was loaded into the back of the ambulance and driven away. When Johnny's father arrived, he parked the car just long enough for Johnny to hop in, and then they drove away too.

Chapter 22

"We live together for a reason," Cryp barked.

Kama flashed her teeth, but it didn't scare Cryp. It never did. "Just leave me alone," Kama snarled.

"Why do you have to make everything so difficult?" Cryp asked, then lunged at her.

The other dogs barked. Having long since outgrown their cages, the dogs now gathered at the front of their kennels for a better view of the fight.

"Down! Down!... Hey, can I get some help in here," Dana yelled. She opened the chain link door and tried to separate the two dogs.

Shannon rushed into the room. She held Cryp's collar while Kama was moved to a separate kennel.

Dana stroked Kama's fur and whispered in her ear until her body stopped trembling. "They can't be left alone like that," Dana said. "It's not safe for her."

Shannon shook her head. "We need puppies. They were supposed to have a litter while I was gone," she said. "The army wants proof that a naturally breeding population is possible before we'll get full funding for the program."

"Just let us bring them on a real mission," Dana said. "If others see what these dogs can do, you'll have way more investors than..."

"No, that means going public. We're not ready for that," Shannon said. "Competitors will copy our innovations once they know what we're doing." Shannon's face had turned red. "They have more money and resources," she continued. "Genetic Valley will have to be fully established in order to compete. We need to take the market by surprise."

"These dogs could be helping a lot of people," Dana muttered. "It's a waste not to let them do something meaningful."

Chapter 23

Earlier in the day, barking and shouts had made Shannon rush out of the Mini Room. In fact, she left in such a hurry that she forgot to latch the door to Congo's cage all the way.

Now it was dark in the laboratory. Congo shimmied up another doorframe and reached for the handle.

Daniel looked down the hallway. "Hurry."

"It's stiffer than the last one," Congo said, dangling from the handle. Congo bounced his body up and down. Each time the lever turned, but never enough for the door to unlatch.

"We're trapped," Daniel said. "It's useless!"

Congo swung his body back and forth as he bounced. The extra momentum made the lever turn a little further. The latch finally clicked. "I think I have it," Congo said. "Pull it open before I slip off."

Daniel put his claws into the crack between the door and the frame. Finally, he felt a groove in the metal. He pulled at the door and it opened. As it did, a security alarm rang throughout the laboratory.

Startled, Congo dropped to the ground. Daniel opened the door far enough for both of them to leave the building. The piercing sound of the alarm faded as the door closed behind them.

"Freedom," Congo said, and they slipped away into the darkness.

Chapter 24

The sun had just risen over Genetic Valley, when Shannon arrived. Two squad cars drove away as she entered the laboratory.

"What's missing?" she asked Dr. Bray.

"Two of the minis are gone. Otherwise, everything's here," he explained. "We still don't think anyone broke in."

Shannon crossed her arms. "How much did they see?"

"They came inside a few minutes, but we told them a worker accidently triggered the alarm."

"How much did the cops see?" Shannon asked more firmly.

Dr. Bray looked to see if anyone was listening. "We kept them away from the important rooms."

Shannon's shoulders lowered. "I assume there's no sign of the minis?"

"We couldn't search for them after telling the police nothing was missing," Dr. Bray said. "They must have gotten out of the building though. Otherwise, the alarm wouldn't have gone off."

Shannon nodded. "Let's get the dogs."

They hurried to what had once been called the "Puppy Room." Dogs barked and pressed their front paws against the kennel doors, rattling the latches.

"Get the GPS collars," Shannon ordered.

"The GPS collars?" Dr. Bray repeated. "Shouldn't we wait for their trainers?"

"Those minis need to be found before somebody sees them."

Shannon opened Kama's cage and grabbed her collar. She led Kama to Dr. Bray. He fastened a leash to her, and then clipped a small black box onto her collar. On the side of the box was a little red light that occasionally blinked on, then off.

After attaching a leash and box to Cryp's collar, they led the dogs to the Mini Room. Two empty cages were taken off the counter and set onto the floor. The humans had Cryp smell the cage that had belonged to Daniel, and Kama smelled the cage that had belonged to Congo.

Within seconds, the dogs found the scent trails. They led the humans through the laboratory and to the door that had set off the alarm. Once outside, the humans unclipped the leashes. Kama and Cryp dashed away. They followed the trail through the experimental gardens and fields. A few minutes later, they disappeared into the pine tree forest that covered the mountains.

Chapter 25

"Hi Grandma, are you feeling better?"

"Yes, I'm just tired," his grandmother said.

"So you'll be home soon?" Johnny asked.

She hesitated. "I don't think so... I'm going to be staying somewhere else."

"What do you mean?" he asked.

His grandmother glanced at Johnny's father, and then looked down at her blankets. "I have cancer Johnny."

"Cancer," Johnny repeated, "but I thought you had a stroke."

"I did, but when the doctor was running tests, she found cancer too. I'm not healthy enough to live on the farm anymore."

"Where will you go?"

"There are some nice nursing homes I'm considering." She gave her grandson a smile, even though the rest of her face didn't look happy.

Johnny became quiet. He tried to process everything that was said. "But who's going to take care of the animals if you're gone?" he asked.

Johnny's grandmother looked around the room as she tried to think of the best way to answer. "Remember the conversation we had before your mother was transferred, the one about change?"

Johnny nodded.

"The farm is going to be sold; the animals too, she said. "Their next owner will take care of them."

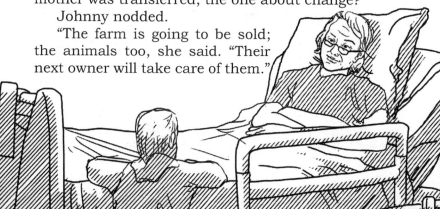

Chapter 26

Two squirrels chased each other along a tree branch but stopped to stare at the strange creatures that were walking across the forest floor.

"Ah, squirrels, the tree dwellers of these forests," Congo said. "Not nearly as intelligent as primates, but they're amazing climbers."

The squirrels lost interest in watching and ran through the treetops once again.

"Why, I could watch them all day," Congo added. "Couldn't you?"

"I could sink my teeth into them. That's for sure," Daniel said, licking his lips.

A bird flittered by, landing on the ground ahead of them.

Daniel crouched. "Here birdie, birdie, birdie."

Congo shook his head. "Carnivores, you're always looking for a poor creature to hunt."

Daniel gave up, as soon as the bird flew further into the forest. "Hey, give me a break," he said. "It's my instinct to hunt."

"But why a beautiful song bird?" Congo asked. "They're such peaceful creatures."

"Why? Cuz I'm the king of the jungle for crying out loud. I'll hunt whatever I want."

"Ha, king of the jungle? If it weren't for humans and their opposable thumbs, gorillas would be king."

Daniel smiled. "You, a king? Maybe I should call you King Kong."

They chuckled at the thought of a mini gorilla with the name King Kong but did not laugh long.

"Did you hear that?" Daniel asked. He stopped walking and turned his ears to listen. His eyes widened. "They're coming." he said, then ran.

Congo picked up his pace to try and keep up. "But we're miles away. You must be..." Before he had a chance to say "mistaken" a distant dog bark echoed through the forest. "No." Congo said. "No. No. No!"

Chapter 27

The faint barking grew louder. Finally, Daniel stopped running and turned to face the dogs.

"Keep going," he said.

Congo stopped. "No. Not without you."

"I said go! At least one of us should be free."

Congo hesitated. Finally, he ran to the closest tree and climbed. Moments later, Cryp leapt over a log. He slowly circled around Daniel.

Daniel stood his ground and roared. He puffed up his mane and tried to look threatening.

Cryp chuckled. He leaned closer. "Well, well, well. Looks like I found a kitten."

"Kitten?" Daniel took a step toward Cryp. He extended his claws and swiped his paw at the dog.

Cryp pulled back just in time. He flashed his teeth. "Bad move. Now, you're going to get it."

"Stop," Kama barked. She jumped over the log and stopped between Cryp and Daniel.

Cryp grabbed Kama by the neck and threw her to the ground. "Whose side are you on?" he growled.

Kama slowly stood. Blood seeped into her fur. "We're supposed to wait," she reminded Cryp. "The humans will decide what to do with him."

"Why don't you worry about your own prisoner," Cryp said, "and I'll worry about mine."

Seeing that Cryp was no longer positioned to attack, Kama lowered her nose to the ground and sniffed. She followed Congo's sent to the tree he was hiding in. "Found you," she said, when she noticed him peering at her from behind a branch.

Chapter 28

Everyone stared at Lav as he and Johnny walked down the hospital hallway. Not far away, Johnny's father carried Lexie in his arms. Lav had never worn a collar or leash before. He had never ridden in a car or been brought into the city before either. Lav trusted Johnny though. Even though he was scared, he knew Johnny would not let anything bad happen to him.

"Is this where you're from Lav?" Lexie asked as they passed a couple doctors. "Are those the people in white coats that used to stick you with needles?"

Lav moved closer to Johnny's side. "They had white coats like that, but they aren't the same people," he said, "and I don't smell any of the other animals here either."

A woman removed a brown purse from her shoulder. She frantically searched through her things. Suddenly, she held up a phone and took a picture of Lav as he passed by.

A moment later, Johnny pulled Lav into a little room. His father and Lexie also entered, and closed the door behind them.

"Hi Grandma," Johnny said. "We brought you some visitors."

"Oh my," she exclaimed.

"I think they missed you," Johnny said.

Lav jumped up and put his front paws onto the old woman's bed. He leaned close to her so she could pet his neck.

"It was Dad's idea to bring them."

"Actually, it was my idea," his grandmother said. "I asked him to bring them here before you take them home with you."

"Home with me," Johnny repeated. He glanced at his father.

"That is if you want to," his grandmother said. "I already talked to your Dad. He said that Lexie and Purple Pup can live with you in the city, as long as you take care of them."

Johnny smiled. "I'll take *good* care of them."

"I know you will." his grandmother said. "You were always a great help with the animals when you visited the farm."

Johnny rubbed behind Lav's ears. "This is going to be so weird."

His grandmother smiled. "It'll be a change for the better."

Chapter 29

"It's about time," Kama said, as the first sound of human voices drifted through the forest.

It was midafternoon and watching the prisoners had become boring. It took another ten minutes before the humans were close enough for Daniel and Congo to hear them too.

"Hide already," Daniel said.

"Quiet," Cryp growled, "or I'll tear you apart."

Congo climbed to the edge of the limb he was sitting on. He grabbed a branch of a neighboring tree. It was a much larger tree, and had a hole in its trunk. He had seen squirrels scurry in and out of the hole throughout the morning.

"Hey," Kama said. "Where do you think you're going?"

Congo climbed to the rim of the hole and peered in. "Mind if I join you?"

Soft chattering resonated from somewhere deep inside the tree.

Congo put his hind legs in first. "Good luck my friend."

"Take care," Daniel said.

Congo slowly lowered himself into the tree. "I'll come back for you. I promise."

The humans appeared a short while later. Cryp's trainer held a GPS and Dana carried two small pet carriers. Dr. Bray was not far behind. He had a gun hanging over his shoulder.

"Looks like they found one," Dr. Bray said. After walking a little closer, he lifted the gun. He aimed at the lion and positioned his finger on the trigger.

Daniel squeezed his eyes closed. "It's alright. Lions are cats. I should have nine lives."

Finally, a shot was fired.

"Oww," Daniel roared. He stared at the dart that had lodged into the side of his body. "Well that wasn't so..." Daniel wobbled back and forth, fell to the ground, and entered into a deep sleep.

Cryp's trainer hooked a leash to Cryp's collar.

"Good job," Cryp's trainer said, as Dr. Bray picked up the lion and set him in a cage.

Dana attached Kama's leash too, but quickly knelt to inspect the bloody fur on Kama's neck.

"This is why I keep telling you not to leave these two dogs alone together," Dana said. She stroked Kama's fur and glared at Dr. Bray.

Dr. Bray shrugged. "They'll have to warm up to each other sooner or later."

"Or else you could be considerate of her wellbeing and use artificial methods," Dana said.

"Trust me; I'd like to start using surrogate mothers. It would be a lot simpler," Dr. Bray said. "But this is the best way to prove they're capable of having puppies on their own."

The humans began to walk back to the laboratory, but Kama and Cryp didn't follow. They pulled their trainers to the tree the gorilla was hiding in.

Cryp leaped into the air. "Don't let him get away," he barked.

"He went in that hole," Kama whined.

The humans stopped and scanned the branches for signs of the gorilla.

"Do you think it's up there?" Dr. Bray asked.

"It has to be there somewhere," Dana said. "Kama wouldn't act this way if it wasn't."

The humans circled the tree, throwing sticks at the branches to scare the gorilla into the open.

"That's enough. At least it ran deeper into the mountains," Dr. Bray finally said. "One mini is better than none. I'll give the GPS coordinates to some of the workers. They can set out traps for it."

The humans began their long walk out of the forest.

"I've got your scent memorized," Cryp shouted. His trainer pulled him further away from the tree. "If you ever cross my path again, I'll kill you."

Chapter 30

After putting Daniel back in the Mini Room, Dr. Bray sat down next to Shannon and began to eat a very late lunch. He was just starting to relax, when Jim appeared in the doorway.

"Hey boss, turn on the news," Jim said. "You'll wanna see this."

Shannon snatched the remote and turned on the television. "What now?" she mumbled.

A picture of Lav appeared on the screen. "I don't believe it," Dr. Bray said.

"Dozens of people in the hospital claim to have seen the purple dog," a news anchor said. "That's right, purple. The photo we're showing you has not been digitally enhanced in any way."

Shannon's face turned red. She held her lips tight together.

Lav's picture disappeared. A reporter and woman with a brown purse appeared on the screen. They were standing in a hospital hallway.

"Hello, I'm Sophia Gral, and beside me is Ann, our original source for this story. She's the person who texted our network a photo of the purple dog, just before witnessing it enter this room."

"It's been so long," Dr. Bray said. "I thought he died, froze to death during the winter."

Sophia suddenly turned around. "It appears someone's leaving... Look! There it is."

The camera zoomed in on Lav, who was trying to hide behind Johnny's legs.

Sophia pointed her microphone at Johnny's father. "Sir, are you the owner of this dog? Is this it's natural fur color?"

Shannon hit the mute button and set the remote back on the table. She stood and paced the room with one hand on her hip and the other over her mouth. "Tell the construction crew that I want them working around the clock," she said. "We're going to be opening sooner than expected. Got it?"

"Sure thing," Dr. Bray said. He rushed out of the room to carry out the orders.

Shannon took her phone out and called a number saved in the contacts. "Russell? It's me. You're watching it too?" She glanced at the television again. "I need you to get that dog back."

Chapter 31

Lav ran from one end of the apartment to the other, before jumping onto the couch.

Lexie lifted her head from the sofa. "Just relax, will you. I'm trying to nap here."

Lav wiggled his body. "Why don't they take us back to the farm?" he asked.

"I told you. I think the boy is our new master. This is our new home."

"But there's no place to run here," Lav whined.

"You love the boy. Don't you?" Lexie asked.

"You know I do."

"Then this is your new home," Lexie said. "He needs us to care for him and bring him happiness."

"I know," Lav said. "But there's nothing to do here."

"Cheer up the boy then. You know he's still sad about the old woman."

Lav ran to the boy and nuzzled his hand.

Johnny stroked the back of Lav's neck. "He's not used to being inside. Can't we just take him for a little walk?"

His dad peeked through the window curtains. Two news station vans were still parked in the street below. "Maybe later this evening," he said "when it's darker outside."

A black vehicle slowed to a stop along the sidewalk. A man stepped out of the car. He wore a nice shirt and carried a manila envelope.

The man walked up to the building. "What now?" Mr. Kantner mumbled.

The man was about to press a button on the buzzer system, but stopped. A woman stepped out of the building. He held the door for her, then entered. A while later there was knocking on their apartment door.

"Hey, what's that noise," Lav shouted to Lexie. He jumped off the couch and ran to the door. "There's someone out there."

"Johnny, can you take him into another room," Mr. Kantner asked.

Lav sniffed the crack between the door and the floor. "I can smell you," Lav barked at the person. Johnny grabbed his collar and pulled him away from the door. "I know you're out there."

Johnny forced Lav into his bedroom, and Mr. Kantner finally opened the door as far as the chain lock would allow.

"Hello, Mr. Kantner," the man said. "My name is Russell, Russell Moreno. I'm here to talk to you about the dog."

Mr. Kantner eased the door shut. "We're not doing interviews."

"The dog has a different owner," Russell blurted.

This time Mr. Kantner unlocked the door and opened it wide enough to get a better look at the man. "What are you talking about?"

"I have paperwork for you to look over," Russell said. He offered the manila envelope. "The dog is a runaway. Now that he's been found, his owner would like him returned, and in a timely manner."

Mr. Kantner's eyebrows narrowed. he accepted the envelope. "Who did you say you were?"

The man pulled a card out of his pocket. "I'm an attorney representing Genetic Pet Shop."

Mr. Kantner glanced at the card. "I've never heard of it before."

Russell smiled. "You have now, and soon the rest of the world will too."

Chapter 32

Lav wagged his tail as Johnny and his dad went for a walk. It was the longest walk he had been on in quite some time.

"It's not fair," Johnny said, as two people approached them.

"I know," Mr. Kantner said, "but this is Purple Pup's real home."

Lav's tail stopped waging. The two humans walking closer smelled familiar. They looked familiar too, but he couldn't tell why.

"Hello. Welcome to Genetic Valley," Shannon said.

Lav growled. He recognized the humans as soon as he heard Shannon's voice. Images of needles and being pinned against the table flooded his memory.

"I'm Shannon, founder and CEO, and this is Dr. Bray, our veterinarian and lead geneticist."

Shannon extended a hand for Mr. Kantner to shake. Lav barked and tried to pull Johnny away from the woman.

Johnny had to lean his body weight to counter Lav's pulling. "Easy boy, it's OK."

"Oh it's so good to see you again," Shannon said, as if she were talking to a baby. She put her hands on her knees and leaned over as she talked. "Don't worry, Lav. I have a treat for you."

"I mean Purple Pup," Shannon quickly said to correct herself. She reached into her side pocket and pulled out a dog biscuit. "We always called him Lav. It was short for Lavender, but I think Purple Pup sounds much better." Shannon gave Johnny a wink, and held the biscuit out for Lav to eat.

Lav stood stand as close to Johnny as possible.

"Are you a little shy? Here you go," Shannon said, and tossed the treat to the ground.

Lav stared at the biscuit. It smelled delicious but he did not eat it. Something didn't seem right.

"Maybe later," Dr. Bray said. "Let's go, we have a lot to show you."

Chapter 33

"This first building is Genetic Pet Shop," Shannon said proudly. "These animals will eventually be in pet shops all around the world."

Johnny's eyes widened as they walked into what looked like a supermarket, except it had aisle upon aisle of cages and aquariums.

"You are now entering the Venomless Aisle," Dr. Bray said. They walked past aquariums containing rattle snakes, cobras, scorpions, and spiders. "These are all child-friendly pets, since they've been designed to have no venom."

Next, they went through the Glow Aisle, which was darkened by a cloth canopy so that the animals would show up better.

"These might just be my favorite," Shannon said. She pointed to a large aquarium that had dozens of glow-in-the-dark butterflies inside. "Isn't it amazing what a little jellyfish DNA can do?"

Eventually, Dr. Bray led them to the next aisle, so he could show everyone a few tricks the mini dolphins had been taught.

"So they caught you too." Daniel said, while the humans watched the miniature aquatic show.

Lav pulled Johnny closer to the lion's cage. "It's you. Where's your gorilla friend?"

"He ran away. Well, we both ran away, but the dogs tracked me down."

"Dogs?"

"Yea, Kama and Cryp," Daniel said.

"Kama...," Lav repeated. "So that's why we came here. The boy is going to bring her home with us. This is going to be awesome." Lav's tail wagged. His body shook with excitement. "Where are they?" Lav asked, as Johnny led him down the aisle.

"Who cares? Look, you got to get out of here before they put you back in a cage too."

"Don't worry. I'm with the boy. He's going to take good care of me."

"Good care of you," Daniel repeated. "He's a human. You can't trust him."

"No, it's alright. The humans outside aren't like the humans here. They take great care of us animals and we take good care of them. It's the best thing in the world."

"Don't say I didn't warn you," Daniel said. Lav and the humans left the aisle. Daniel shook his head. "More proof that cats are smarter than dogs."

Shannon led them down Aisle 7. "I think you'll find this section a little familiar," she said.

On the left side, puppies of all different colors yelped and press their paws against the front of their cages. Some even had different colored spots, patches, and stripes on them. To the right, different colored kittens pounced on one another and licked their fur.

"All of these animals were genetically engineered to be extraordinary pets," Shannon continued. She pulled a puppy with leopard spotted fur out of its cage and held it against the side of her face. "And just like Purple Pup, most of them have chinchilla genes to make their fur soft."

"Look dad," Johnny said, as Lav sniffed a cage that had seven green puppies inside.

Mr. Kantner smiled back.

Just above the cage with green puppies was an empty cage, with a sign that read, "Purple Puppies."

Johnny pointed to the cage. "Why aren't there any in this one?" he asked.

"Our goal was to get a breeding pair for each of the dogs that we created," Dr. Bray said. "Since Purple Pup hasn't been here, we haven't had any purple puppies born."

"But that will change soon now that he's back," Shannon said, as she returned the leopard spotted puppy to its cage.

"But why can't you just make another purple dog. Why can't Purple Pup stay with me?"

"Johnny, we talked about this," Mr. Kantner said.

Shannon knelt so that she could be at eye level with Johnny. "Trust me, making a purple dog is difficult. It's not cheap either. After we get some samples from Purple Pup and he proves that natural reproduction is possible, he's going to have to be sterilized and sold."

"Sterilized," Johnny repeated.

"We'll give him a shot so that he won't be able to have puppies," Dr. Bray explained.

"You mean *never*?"

Shannon shook her head. "None of the animals we sell will be able to have offspring."

Johnny narrowed his eyebrows. "Why would you do that?"

"It's only fair. Isn't it? Shouldn't we be the only ones to breed and sell the animals we create?" Shannon smiled. "I know you think of them as pets, but to us, they're more like inventions."

"They're patent pending," Dr. Bray added.

The tension on Johnny's face remained.

Shannon stood up. "Johnny, don't look at me like I'm an evil villain." She turned and continued to walk down the aisle. "Come on, there's something in particular I want to show you."

Chapter 34

Shannon led them out of the Pet Shop and into a building shaped like a giant barn. The sign above the doorway read "Genetic Farmyard."

"These cows make milk with additional vitamins in it," she said. "Those sheep grow extra warm wool... Those pigs produce heart healthy meat, which is quite tasty I assure you... These chickens will make it so that people won't need to get shots anymore. Eating their eggs will provide you with the vaccinations for the most common diseases...and each of these horses are faster than any that you'll find at this year's Kentucky Derby."

Finally, they made it to the back of the barn and passed through a door that led into a large dome-shaped greenhouse. Inside, it looked like a massive garden, full of many different plants.

"These watermelons are extra sweet...those carrots are better for your eyes than regular ones... These potatoes are frost and insect resistant..."

Finally, Shannon did something a little different. She walked up to a vine, tore off a cluster of grapes, and handed it to Johnny. "Can you guess what these are designed to do?"

Johnny looked at the grapes before shaking his head. "What?"

"They produce high levels of seven different compounds that have been clinically proven to help prevent the growth of tumors. Our research shows that when animals eat these grapes on a regular basis, they are 70% less likely to develop cancers, much like the one your grandmother has."

Johnny's lip quivered. Shannon stepped closer. She was about to put a hand on his shoulder but stopped when Lav began to growl. "Johnny, I'm sorry that I mentioned your grandmother's condition. I just want you to see that what we are doing here is trying to make people's lives better."

"And Purple Pup is going to help us do that." Dr. Bray added. "The money from his sale will help us continue our research. That way we can keep inventing things to prevent, and maybe cure all sorts of diseases."

"It's going to be years, maybe decades before we get approval for people to eat most of the food we grow. That's why we're relying on Genetic Pet Shop to pay our bills, and quite honestly, now that we need to open early, we're running short on money," Shannon continued.

Johnny bit his bottom lip.

"In a perfect world, we wouldn't need to take Purple Pup back," Shannon said, "Unfortunately, this is just part of doing business."

"Can I still come and visit him?" Johnny asked.

Shannon nodded. "Of course, any time you like."

Chapter 35

Kama and Cryp were working with their trainers. Kama was in the process of following a scent trail, when a another smelled caught her attention.

"It can't be." She sniffed more. "Lav?... Lav," she barked, and sprinted in the direction of his smell.

Dana blew a whistle signaling Kama to return, but Kama kept running. The other trainer grabbed Cryp's collar in case he was tempted to run too.

"Kama," Cryp barked. "Get back here."

Kama dashed around the laboratory. When she rounded the far corner of the building she could finally see him.

"Lav," she barked.

After Lav realized who was shouting his name he tried to run toward her, but the leash pulled tight around his neck.

When Kama reached Lav, they bounced around and nipped at each other's ears, just like old times. "Lav, I thought I'd never see you again," she said.

"Wow Kama, you look so grown up," Lav said.

Kama shook her head. "Look who's talking."

"This is going to be great. You can live with us now. The boy is a lot of fun. You're going to love him. Just wait until I show you how to play fetch."

Finally, Shannon was able to grab Kama's collar. She held on tight until Dana caught up.

"It looks like these two know each other," Mr. Kantner said. "Is that possible?"

"I'm sure they do. They would have grown up in the same room together," Dr. Bray said.

Johnny held out his hand for Kama to smell, then began to pet her back. "Can I see where Purple Pup will live?" he asked.

Chapter 36

They followed Dana and Kama through the laboratory. Dr. Bray pointed out different rooms and explained what experiments were taking place in each of them.

"What's in this room?" Johnny asked, when he noticed only one had its door closed.

"Nothing, just cleaning supplies." Dr. Bray said.

Johnny took a few steps closer. "It sounds like a baby crying in there."

Dr. Bray glanced at Shannon. Shannon smiled and Dr. Bray let out a chuckle.

"In a laboratory like this, you never know," Shannon said. "Now let's go, I have a meeting that'll be starting soon."

Memories raced through Lav's mind, as they continued down the hall. He recognized the white walls, the smell of the cleaning chemicals, and the musty odors. Eventually they walked through an open doorway. An explosion of barking erupted as they entered the room.

"Hey, look who Kama found. It's Lav."

"Where've you been?"

"What you're not too good for us anymore?"

"What's it like on the outside Lav?"

"This one's his," Dr. Bray said, pointing to a kennel that had one purple dog in it.

"Well, well. Didn't you grow up nice," Violetta said.

Lav followed Johnny into the kennel. Lav looked around. The other kennels had two dogs in them. Two green, two red, two orange, and him and Violetta made a kennel with two purple dogs.

Johnny knelt beside Lav and gave him a hug. "I love you Purple Pup. I'll be back to visit tomorrow. I promise."

Lav tried to leave the kennel with Johnny, but the boy only opened the door wide enough for himself to slip out. The door closed and locked behind him.

"Where are you going? Take me with you," Lav whined.

Johnny and the other people walked back into the hallway.

"Wait! Come back," Lav barked.

Before he was out of sight, Johnny looked over his shoulder one last time. Lav could see tear streaks glistening on the boy's face.

Chapter 37

"Hello. Welcome to the evening news. I'm Sophia Gral. For those of you who haven't heard, Genetic Valley is the research facility claiming to have created Purple Pup. We covered that story yesterday, and since that time viewers have been flooding our website with comments.

We asked Genetic Valley's founder and CEO, Shannon Huber for an interview, but she sent Russell Moreno instead. He's the company's attorney and official spokesperson. Hopefully, he can clear up some of the biggest questions we have. Welcome to the show."

"Thank you Sophia."

"Now, Mr. Moreno, many people are excited about the work Genetic Valley is doing with genetically modified organisms, also known as GMOs, but as you can see by the protesters gathering in front of Genetic Valley, plenty of people are strongly opposed. Some of their concerns include the environmental impact this may have and the ethics of modifying animals. What do you have to say to these skeptics?"

"I'd like to remind them that people have been modifying organisms for thousands of years. Throughout recorded history, crops have been cultivated and animals have been bred to obtain desirable genetic traits. Genetic Valley is simply using technology to speed up this process."

"But is there a difference between manipulating DNA and modifying it? It seems that engineering a dog to have purple fur is beyond the capabilities of dog breeding."

Mr. Moreno nodded. "There are some differences. Purple Pup, for instance, has genes from a violet plant incorporated into his DNA."

"A violet? Really," Sophia said. "I don't suppose he smells like a flower too."

"No, he was only given the genes needed to produce purple pigment."

"Now mixing and matching DNA from different species is nothing new is it," Sophia said. "Other companies have been doing this for decades. What makes Genetic Valley different?"

"You're right. People have been doing this for years," Mr. Moreno said, "but under Shannon's leadership, Genetic Valley has invested heavily in developing the best Phenotype Prediction Software in the world."

"Phenotype Prediction Software," Sophia repeated. "Could you explain that for us?"

"To put it simply, all we need to do is enter a DNA sequence into our computer and a fairly accurate simulation of what that plant or animal would look like will appear on the screen. Other companies still spend most of their time on trial and error methods of testing."

"With technology like this, I'm sure Genetic Valley is doing more than just making purple dogs,"

Sophia said. "What other animals have been created?"

"That's a great question Sophia, but unfortunately I'm not allowed to release that information. The best way for people to learn about our other creatures is by coming to the Grand Opening of Genetic Pet Shop, which is scheduled for the end of the month.

Chapter 38

Lav threw himself against the sides of the kennel and barked.

"Calm down. It's going to be alright," Kama said.

"I have to get out of here. The boy needs me."

"Needs you? He left you here," Cryp said.

"But he didn't want to. He was crying. Something isn't right," Lav said. He barked even louder.

Violetta had been trying to sleep, but suddenly sat up. "Seriously, just shut up for a while. I forgot how annoying you are."

"But, I'm not supposed to be here."

"Of course you are. You were never *supposed* to run away." Violetta said. "We should have had puppies a long time ago."

"Puppies? Me and you? Why would we have puppies?"

Violetta rolled her eyes. "Because that's what we're *supposed* to do."

"But we don't even like each other," Lav said.

"That doesn't matter," Cryp barked. "The humans put you two together for a reason. Look around. Two red dogs together to make red puppies, two orange dogs together to make orange puppies, and now that you're back there are two purple dogs to make purple puppies. You two are meant to be together." Cryp turned to Kama's kennel. "Just like we're meant to be together," he said.

Lav finally sat down. "So you guys really had puppies?" he asked.

"Yea, except Cryp and Kama," a red dog said.

A blue dog began to wag its tail. "We actually had the first litter."

"But we had the biggest," a yellow dog bragged, "eleven puppies in ours."

"Why haven't you had any?" Lav asked Kama, but she set her head on the floor and didn't answer.

"Mind your own business," Cryp barked.

Violetta leaned closer to Lav. "Kama doesn't want puppies and Cryp does. They fight about it a lot. That's why they're in separate kennels. Every time the humans make them live together, Cryp loses his temper and Kama gets hurt."

Chapter 39

The other dogs had been sleeping for hours. Lav was the only one awake. He stared at the fire alarm on the wall. Its blinking light was sadly familiar. It almost felt like he had never left the laboratory.

Kama lifted her head. Her ears perked higher than normal. She sniffed the air. A moment later Cryp began to growl.

"What do you hear?" Lav asked.

"He's got some nerve to show up here again," Cryp said. "This time I'll rip him to pieces."

"Why are you so surprised?" Kama asked. "He said he'd come back for the lion."

"Lion," Lav repeated. "Who's out there?"

"Another runaway," Cryp snarled.

"A little gorilla," Kama said.

"Gorilla," Lav repeated. He ran to the front of his cage. "Congo. It's me, Lav. Congo!"

Lav's barking woke the other dogs, but they didn't bother to lift their heads from the floor until Congo appeared in the doorway. Then they sprang to their feet and barked as well.

"What are you doing here?" Congo asked Lav.

"I don't know, but you got to get me out."

"Lav, don't," Kama said. "You just came back."

"Once a runaway, always a runaway," Cryp growled.

"I'm looking for Daniel," Congo explained. "He's not in the Mini Room. None of the minis are."

"I know. They have him in a different building," Lav said. "I saw him. I can show you the way."

With all the dogs barking Congo knew he didn't have much time. He climbed up the wire fencing on

the kennel door and lifted the metal latch. "There, now push," Congo said.

Lav pressed against the door. It swung open.

Congo kept a close eye on Violetta. He pushed the kennel door closed again. "Alright, which way is he?" Congo asked.

"Wait a minute," Lav said. He trotted up to Kama's kennel. "Can you get her out too?"

Kama moved to the back of her kennel and sat down. "No, I can't" she said. "I'm not a runaway."

"But you tried running away with me when we were younger," Lav said. "Remember, we were going to live outside and be free."

"That was a long time ago. I have a trainer now. This is where I belong."

"How do you know that?" Lav asked. "Have you ever been anywhere else? I've found a wonderful place to live, and a boy who takes great care of animals. The only thing that could make it better would be having you there too."

"There's no time for this," Congo scolded.

"Remember when I tried to let you out when I was a puppy," Lav asked.

Congo nodded.

"Would you have left without Daniel?"

Congo didn't answer.

"Kama's my friend," Lav pleaded.

Congo hesitated. "Alright, but let's hurry."

"Don't you dare," Cryp barked, as Congo climbed Kama's kennel. Cryp jumped against the fencing. "I'll kill you. I'll tear you to shreds."

"Let's go Kama," Lav said. "This is our chance."

"But I'm scared. I've never lived anywhere else," she said.

Congo lifted the latch to Kama's door. "You'll have to push if you want to get out."

"Look, if you're happy living here, stay," Lav said, "But if not, come with us."

Kama's body shook, yet she slowly walked to the front of her kennel.

"Don't Kama," Cryp shouted, but she pushed the door with her nose. "You're better than them. We're better than them. We're supposed to be together!"

"But we don't even love each other," Kama said. "You just love with the idea of us being together."

"But look at our fur," Cryp shouted. "We're a pair, the perfect pair."

"Goodbye Cryp," Kama said, before following Lav and Congo into the hallway.

Chapter 40

Congo climbed the door frame and grabbed onto the handle. "Once this door opens an alarm is going to sound," he explained. "We'll only have minutes after that, so we'll need to hurry."

Lav nodded.

The gorilla swung his body back and forth. He yanked on the handle until a clicking noise was heard.

"Alright," Congo said. He continued to dangle from the handle. "Can you pull it open?"

Lav tried to claw at the door, but his claws were too big to get into the crack between the door and the frame.

Kama stood up on her hind legs and put her paws onto the wall. Congo watched nervously as Kama opened her mouth and leaned closer to him. Her jaws closed on the door handle, just above his hands, and she pulled.

The door opened a few inches, but that was all it took to set off the alarm. It was also just enough space for Lav's paws to grab the door. He pulled it the rest of the way open and the three animals dashed out of the laboratory.

"That's the one," Lav said. He led the way to a second building. All the windows to the building were dark, but there was one large light illuminating the sign that read "Genetic Pet Shop."

"Alright you two, wait here," Congo said. He climbed a drainage pipe that was running down an outside wall. "Believe it or not, it's harder breaking into these buildings than it is to break out of them," he added, before disappearing on the roof.

Humans were gathering around the laboratory, so Lav and Kama hid behind some bushes.

"Stop shaking so much," Lav said. "We're outside. We're free now. The humans are too slow to catch us."

"It's not the humans I'm worried about," Kama said. "Cryp won't just let me run away like this. I'm sure he's furious right now."

"Don't worry about Cryp," Lav said. "I won't let him hurt you anymore."

"He's strong," Kama said. "Even stronger than when we were puppies."

A few minutes later, lights turned on inside of Genetic Pet Shop. Lav could hear all the animals calling and yelling. It sounded like a huge commotion inside. Eventually he could hear Jim shouting too.

Lav tilted his head to the side. "I remember him."

"He's still the one human that brings us food," Kama said.

The door to Genetic Pet Shop opened. Daniel and Congo rushed out. They were followed by other animals too. An oversized rabbit darted past them. A venomless rattle snake slithered into the grass. Illumiflies fluttered through the top of the doorway, and danced into the night sky.

"What did you do?" Lav asked, as they ran toward the forest with Congo and Daniel.

"I opened as many animal cages as I could," Congo said. "Hopefully the humans will be too distracted to track us down like last time."

"It's not the humans you have to worry about," Kama said.

Lav shook his head. "There's two of us. Together, we're stronger than he is."

"Don't be so sure," Kama warned

Chapter 41

Dr. Bray, Shannon, Jim, and the trainers hurried down the hallway.

"What do you mean she's gone?" Dana asked.

Shannon rolled her eyes. "What do you think I mean?"

"First, you release our dogs to find other missing animals. Now you're missing a dog too... This is some facility you're running," Dana said.

Shannon's eyes widened and her lips tightened. "It would run a lot smoother if we had all of the funding that was promised."

"Yea, well you promised two dogs and some puppies," Cryp's trainer said, as they entered the dog room.

"There will be two dogs and some puppies once Cryp finds her," Shannon insisted. "All the other dogs were able to have puppies. There's no reason the hunting dogs can't."

Cryp waited as a GPS was attached to his collar. The humans took him to Kama's cage for scent. He didn't need to smell her scent though. He was just waiting for permission to begin.

"Go find her," his trainer said.

Cryp dashed into the hallway and the trainers left the room. Shannon turned and glared at Jim. "You didn't tell me Lav is missing too."

Jim shifted his feet. "I know. I was getting to that."

"You're in charge of making sure the animals are locked up and safe," Shannon said. "I'm sure you understand that I'll have to let you go."

"But they were locked up," Jim protested. He fiddled with the large ring of keys attached to his belt. "There's nothing else I could have done."

"This is the second time you've let Lav get away, not to mention Kama and all the other animals that got out last night too. I'm sorry, but you're fired."

Jim lowered his head. "Yes ma'am." He unhooked the ring of keys from his belt. He handed them to Shannon, then left the room.

Shannon held her fingertips against her forehead. "I should have done that a long time ago."

Chapter 42

As the sun rose, chattering drifted from the treetops. Soon squirrels could be seen jumping from one tree limb to another.

"I told you I'd be back," Congo said to the squirrels.

Daniel shook his head. "Seriously, you have squirrel friends now?"

"They're amazing creatures," Congo said. "Their intelligence might be lacking, but they have outstanding memories. The squirrels have nuts and seeds hidden all over this forest, and somehow they remember where they are."

"Wait," Kama said, and everyone stopped. She held her nose high and sniffed the air. "There's a dog up ahead."

"Cryp?" Congo asked.

"No, a stranger."

Daniel tucked his tail close to his body. He crouched lower to the ground. "I have a bad feeling about this."

Kama's ears perked higher. "There's more," she said. Her eyes widened and she turned to look in the direction they had been running from. "They're surrounding us."

Although Lav couldn't hear or smell anything unusual, he stepped closer to Kama and growled.

"Man, what a nose," a voice called out. A moment later a black wolf lifted his head and walked into the open. "We were down wind and everything," he said.

As the wolf walked closer, a large scar on the side of his snout became visible. Soon other wolves left their hiding spots too. Kama was right, they were surrounded.

"Leave us alone," Lav growled. "We're just passing through."

"Yea, passing through our hunting grounds," a different wolf snarled.

She took a few steps closer to Lav. The way she was crouched low to the ground made it look like she was going to attack at any moment.

"Relax Tehya," the black wolf commanded.

Tehya backed away from Lav and sat down.

"I'm Nanook, the leader of this pack," the black wolf explained. He bowed his head and smiled. "Normally we kill domestics that wonder into our territory, but I'd like to make you a special offer."

"And what's that?" Lav asked.

"Well sorry, it's actually a deal for the lady," Nanook said, before addressing Kama more specifically. "The pack could use someone with a sense of smell like yours. What do you think about joining?"

"Forget it," Lav said. "The farm animals told me stories about wolves. You can't trust them Kama."

"Farm animals," Nanook repeated. "They're the worst kind of domestics. You don't know anything about wolves or what it means to be a canine."

"Come on, let's get out of here," Lav said. He intended to walk past Nanook, but came to a quick stop when three other wolves stepped in his way.

"So are you asking me to join, or are you telling me to join?" Kama asked.

"In the wild, a canine is free to do whatever it wants," Nanook said, "but naturally there are consequences for one's choices."

The three wolves began to growl at Lav. They continued to do so until Lav took a few steps closer to Kama.

"Alright then," Kama said. "I'll join under one condition."

"And what's that?" Nanook asked.

"You promise safety for me and my friends."

"Of course," Nanook said. "Anyone who joins the pack receives the protection of the pack."

"Does that include my friends too?"

Nanook looked at Lav and the two minis. "Tonight is a full moon," he said. "Be our tracker until the next full moon comes, and you have yourself a deal."

Chapter 43

Mrs. Kantner leaned closer to her computer screen. She watched her son sit down at the end of his grandmother's bed.

"We shouldn't have left him there," Johnny said.

The video shook while Mr. Kantner pulled one of the hospital chairs closer to the bed too. Finally, he held the phone far enough away from his body so that he and Johnny would show up in the video chat again.

"It doesn't really sound like you had a choice," Mrs. Kantner said. "He's their dog."

"No he's not. They never even looked for him or hung up signs saying that he was missing. Me and

Grandma have been taking care of him since he was a puppy." Johnny turned to look at his grandma. She was still sleeping. She had slept a lot the last couple days and was usually tired while awake too.

"Maybe you were lucky to spend that much time with Purple Pup," Mr. Kantner said. "Besides, he didn't like living in the city. Genetic Valley is probably a better home for him now."

"My contract is going to be finished in a couple months," Mrs. Kantner said. "As soon as I get transferred back home we can pick out a new dog."

"Maybe a smaller, house dog," Mr. Kantner added.

Johnny didn't say anything. Tear drops rolled off his face and his bottom lip trembled.

"Johnny," Mrs. Kantner said. "I know a new dog won't be the same, but…"

"Nothing is the same," Johnny said. "Everything's changed. Purple Pup is gone, grandma is sick and selling the farm, and you don't even live here anymore. I hate it."

Chapter 44

Cryp sprinted through the forest. The scent trail was more than easy to follow. Technically, it was four trails in one. Cryp hardly paid attention to the scent of the minis or any other odors for that matter. It was the smell of Lav and Kama walking side-by-side that infuriated him.

He couldn't understand why Lav and Kama were traveling with the minis. The minis were just slowing them down. Their legs were too small for them to travel as fast as a full-sized dog. With every passing minute, the odors on the trail grew stronger and stronger. It meant that he was gaining on them. Soon he would be able to have his revenge, first on Lav, then on the minis.

Finally, Cryp could hear their voices.

"He's coming," Kama said.

Cryp slowed down to an easy trot. He wanted to catch his breath before any fighting took place.

"Anybody else smell him?" Nanook asked.

"Nothing... Nope... I think she's pulling your tail..." voices responded.

Cryp stopped for a moment. He didn't recognize Nanook's voice or any of the other strangers that he heard. For the next few minutes, he followed the trail more cautiously.

"Wait a minute," a voice said. "I smell him."

"Kama," Cryp barked, once he came in sight. "It's time to go back."

"I'm not going anywhere," Kama said.

Cryp came to a stop when he reached the group. "I'm not asking you if you want to or not. You *are* coming back with me."

"Didn't you hear her," Daniel said. "She's not going anywhere."

"You stay out of this," Cryp barked, and bolted toward the lion.

Three of the wolves leaped forward and one plowed into the side of Cryp's body. The attack surprised him, but Cryp quickly rolled back onto his feet. He growled at the wolves while they circled around him.

"Who are these strangers?" Cryp asked.

"Our new friends," Kama said.

"Once in the pack, you're more like family," Nanook corrected.

"Just leave," Kama said. "I don't want you to get hurt."

"My orders were to find you," Cryp said "and I'm not leaving without you."

Nanook walked closer to Cryp. "Am I correct to assume that you can hear and smell as well as Kama."

"That's right," Cryp said.

"I can tell you're strong. We need strength to capture our prey. Will you join our pack too?"

"No," Lav said, "That wasn't a part of the deal. You were supposed to chase him away from us."

Nanook glared at Lav. "The deal was to protect you. Whether we chase him away or welcome him into the pack is up to me."

Cryp looked at the wolves. There were too many for him to fight.

"What's your answer?" Nanook asked. "Hunt with us or return to your humans."

"I'll hunt, as long as Kama's with the pack."

"Deal," Nanook said. "Alright, back to the den everyone."

Nanook led the pack into the forest but paused before passing Kama. He sprang at her and bit at her neck. Two wolves stepped in front of Lav as Nanook thrashed his head hard enough to make Kama fall to the ground.

"You won't be needing this," Nanook said, as he let Kama's broken collar drop from his mouth. "Someone please help Cryp and Lav with theirs."

A wolf latched onto Lav's collar and threw him to the ground too. Then Lav hurried over to Kama. "Are you alright?" he asked.

Cryp growled as one of the three wolves that had attacked him earlier stepped closer.

"Relax tuff guy," Tehya said.

Her voice surprised Cryp. He hadn't realized she was a girl wolf. He stopped growling and tightened his muscles as she took his collar between her teeth. Cryp stumbled a few times as she thrashed her head. Eventually, the collar snapped. Then it was tossed beside a pinecone. The light on the little black box continued to blink on and off.

Cryp followed the wolves past Kama. "When this is all over, you're coming back to the lab with me."

Kama didn't say anything as he walked by.

"I'll drag you back if I need to," he added.

He glanced at Lav and the Minis. A toothy grin appeared on Cryp's face. He winked at them, then followed the pack into the forest.

Daniel's ears drooped. "He's going to kill me."

Part 3

The Wild

Chapter 45

"Tonight, your job is to help us find our prey; to prove yourselves as trackers," Nanook told Cryp and Kama, as the pack waited for the full moon to rise. "Hunting is more complicated. For now, watch how we work together to make a kill. Hopefully, in a few nights, you can *all* join us as hunters."

Lav could tell by the way Nanook emphasized "all" that it included him too.

"There is no greater honor than to hunt and serve your fellow pack members," Nanook continued. "It's what the creator made canines to do."

"I thought the creator made dogs to serve humans," Lav said.

"Serve humans," Nanook repeated. "When the creator made the world, he made everything in nature balanced. It's humans who ruin this balance."

"That's not true," Lav said. "Most humans are great."

"Yea real great," Nanook said. "They made buildings in the valley and turned the meadows into farmland. Now the deer have nowhere to graze. Their herds keep getting smaller. Too many of them are starving."

"Fewer deer means less for us to eat too." Tehya said. She bowed her head. "The pack is half the size it was before the humans came to the valley."

"Not all humans are like the ones in the valley," Lav said. "I used to hate humans too. Then I met a boy. Serving him is the best thing in the world. I'd do anything to make sure he's safe and happy."

Nanook and most of the pack members laughed.

"Just shut up, will you," Cryp muttered.

"No, it's true," Lav said. "You don't know what it's like."

"You're right. I don't know what it's like, and I don't want to," Nanook said. "There was a time when all canines were free, and a part of nature's balance. Then the humans came. They offered our ancestors food. It seemed like a generous gift, but it was a terrible trick. The ones who took the food no longer had to hunt, and they slowly forgot how. After that, they had no choice but to obey human commands, and since that time, hundreds of breeds of domestics have formed..."

"All willing to sit and roll over if it means another doggy treat tossed to the floor," Tehya said.

The rest of the pack chuckled some more.

"Humans only take care of animals so that they can control them," Nanook said.

"It's not like that," Lav insisted. "The boy loves me."

"Then why did the boy leave you?" Cryp asked.

Lav glanced at the full moon rising above the mountain side. He didn't quite know how to answer.

"Because humans can't be trusted," Nanook finally said. He trotted up a hill and looked down at his pack. "Deep in every canine's soul is the desire to be free. It takes brains and talent to stay alive in the wilderness. It's not an easy life, like the one humans provide, but it's the only life worth living."

Nanook tilted his head backward and let out a long, slow howl. A short while later, others in the pack howled too. It sent shivers down Lav's spine and into the very core of his body.

Finally, Nanook and the others stopped.

"Tonight, we'll help your hearts remember how to be free."

With those words, Nanook led the pack into the forest and the newest members were not far behind.

Daniel squirmed beneath a rock pile. He struggled through a thin gap in the stones. It was the only place he felt safe from Cryp and the wolves.

Daniel extended his front legs and stretched his back. He held this position a moment, then allowed his claws to slide out of his front paws.

He jumped from the rocks. "Let the hunt begin."

"Good luck," Congo said.

Daniel lurked the into forest and disappeared in the shadows.

Chapter 46

The canines returned as the first light appeared in the eastern sky. Although everything was still dim in the forest, Daniel could see blood stains on the pack's faces. The hunt had been a success.

"That was too easy," Tehya said to Cryp as they entered the den. "With a sense of smell like yours we can pinpoint every deer on the mountain."

"Smelling is simple," Cryp said. "I want a turn at hunting. That deer was fast. I thought it was going to get away for sure, but the way you all surrounded it. Man, that was awesome."

"I could show you some takedown moves if you want," Tehya said.

"Takedown moves?"

"Yea, there's a few tricks that makes taking them down a lot easier."

"I like the sound of that," Cryp said.

Kama walked out of the forest with Lav. Her face was not as bloody as the others. "I can't believe I ate that poor creature," she said.

"Don't feel bad," Lav reassured her. "It's just the way things are in the wild."

"But I'm not a normal tracker. I can smell things other dogs can't. How are deer supposed to hide from me? It didn't have a fair chance."

"You did what you had to," Lav said. "Besides, meat is meat. Where do you think the humans get theirs?...pigs, chickens, and even cows like Daisy. Farm animals are meant to be food for humans, just like deer are meant to be food for the wolves."

"Let's go back to the valley," Kama whimpered.

Lav glanced at the den to make sure nobody was listening to them. "Go back? But we need to find the farm and the boy. Besides, you made a deal with Nanook. If they catch us running away..."

"But I hate living in the forest," Kama said, before drooping her ears.

Daniel licked his lips as they came closer to the stone he was resting on. "That smells delicious."

"It wasn't bad," Lav said. "What did you catch?"

Daniel stretched his jaws open and yawned. "Those rabbits are too fast."

"They aren't your natural prey," Congo said, from a tree branch above them. He carefully broke apart a pine cone and put one of the pine nuts in his mouth. A squirrel crawled beside Congo and chattered, until he handed it one of the nuts. The squirrel tucked it in the side of its mouth, and then scurried down the tree trunk.

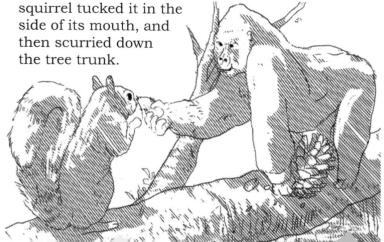

"Yea, I bet that's my problem," Daniel said. "Hey, if you see a mini zebra or gazelle running around, let me know."

"I'll do that," Lav said. "But just in case, I'll bring back a piece of meat for you next time."

"Have I ever mentioned how much I like you?" Daniel asked. Then he crawled into the stone pile for a cat nap.

"What is it?" Lav asked, when he noticed the way Kama was sniffing the air.

Kama didn't answer. She seemed to be listening to something. Her tail started to wag. Soon, Cryp stepped out of the den too. He was also holding his nose higher than normal.

"Humans," Cryp told the others, "ones from the valley."

"But humans never come to this part of the mountain," Tehya said.

"They're looking for us," Cryp explained.

"Everyone in the den, and keep quiet," Nanook ordered. "If they get close, we'll move out."

"Who is it?" Lav asked.

Kama smiled. "It's my trainer. She's calling my name."

Nanook realized that Kama and Lav were not following orders. "I said in the den," he growled.

"Come on," Lav said. "We only need to live here a little while. Then we can go find the farm."

Kama's tail sagged between her legs and her head drooped closer to the ground as she and Lav reluctantly joined the others.

Chapter 47

"Due to routine maintenance to the facility, we're not accepting visitors at..." Shannon had to stop talking because the person on the other end of the phone began to yell. She glanced at the protesters gathering at the main entrance to Genetic Valley. There were even more people than the day before.

"I know I said that, but this is an exception. Johnny can visit Purple Pup once we are up and running again."

Shannon lowered the phone away from her ear as a man in an army uniform appeared. He had an emotionless facial expression.

"Sorry Mr. Kantner. I need to go," Shannon said, and quickly hung up the phone. "Why Lieutenant Kimbal, what a pleasant surprise."

Lieutenant Kimbal did not return her smile. "I wanted to analyze this situation myself."

"Oh, this is just a minor setback," Shannon said. She gestured to all the workers searching the fields and edges of the forest. "Our animals don't know how to find food in the wild. Most of them have already been recaptured at the bait stations."

"Not the dogs," Lieutenant Kimbal pointed out.

"No but, well, hang on a second," Shannon said, because she noticed Dana walking in their direction. Shannon hurried toward her but stopped when she saw the way Dana's eyebrows were narrowed. "Any luck?" Shannon asked.

"This is what you get for having them track the minis by themselves." Dana said. She tossed something by Shannon's feet. It was Kama's torn collar. "Kama would have never run away before that." Dana tossed two more collars onto the ground.

"I think I've seen enough," Lieutenant Kimbal said. "I'm terminating all funding for this program."

"Now let's not make any drastic decisions," Shannon said, in a failed attempt to keep him from leaving. "Let's at least talk this over."

Lieutenant Kimbal stopped and turned back around. "Dana, come with me. I'm going to find you a new assignment."

"But sir, with all due respect..." Dana paused now that the Lieutenant was standing with his back a little straighter. "The dogs are fully trained. They're ready for missions in the field."

"I'm as disappointed as you are," the Lieutenant said, "but it's time to pack your things. We're done here."

Chapter 48

"This way," Cryp said. The pack trotted close behind him. "They're on the other side of that hill."

"How many?" Nanook asked.

"Five," Kama said. She sniffed the air some more. "Two of them are fawns though."

"Perfect," Nanook said. "A fawn will make an easy first kill for you beginners."

"I couldn't," Kama said. "Especially not a *fawn.*"

"Don't look at me like that," Nanook said. "This is our way of keeping balance in the forest. We weed out the weakest animals, and the strongest are left to survive. Now let's go."

Nanook and half of the pack left to circle around the hill. The others looked for good places to hide. Since Cryp and Tehya usually hung out together, they crouched behind the same bush. Kama found a wide based tree to stand behind. Then Lav laid down next to a log.

Lav had seen the pack hunt enough times to know that Nanook's group wasn't intending to attack the deer. They were going to chase them over the hill and into the jaws of those that were hiding.

"Remember what I taught you," Tehya whispered to Cryp. "Aim for their neck."

"And steer clear of their hooves," Cryp finished. "I know."

Cryp's ears perked up. So did Kama's.

"What is it?" Tehya asked.

"Growling and hoof beats," Cryp said. "They're almost here."

A few moments later, the deer bounded over the crest of the hill. The fawns couldn't leap as high as the larger deer, and their eyes seemed to bulge with fright. Nanook and the others appeared at the top of the hill too.

At first, it looked like the deer were going to run right into the ambush. Then, all the deer except one changed direction. Only the smallest fawn continued straight down the hill.

"It's headed right for you," Nanook called, as the fawn rushed closer to where Lav was hiding.

The fawn came to a stop. It stared at Lav. Then looked in the direction the other deer had run.

Lav stood up and took a few running strides closer to the fawn, but stopped when Kama said, "Lav, don't."

"Attack," Nanook yelled.

Lav hesitated.

The fawn seemed to give up the thought of rejoining the others and ran in a different direction.

"Come on," Tehya said to Cryp, when she saw Lav let the fawn get away.

They sprang forward and ran side by side after the other four deer.

Tehya realized Cryp wasn't following the last fawn. "What are you doing?" she asked.

Cryp barked at the largest deer. Tehya began trailing the large deer too and helped Cryp chase it from the rest of the herd. The two canines and the deer disappeared in a tangle of branches. Cryp's barks continued to echo through the forest, until his barking turned to growls. Then there was silence.

"Lav, what happened?" Nanook shouted. He trotted down the hill with the other wolves. "You let it escape."

"Make him stay back at the den next time," a different wolf said. "He sticks out too much. Those other deer noticed him right away."

Lav hadn't felt so ashamed of his fur since the cows had teased him many months ago. Purple wasn't a good color for blending in with the trees. The wolves and even Kama and Cryp looked natural in the forest. Now Lav felt like an outsider. He felt like the pack was upset with him too.

"And what about you Kama?" Nanook asked. "You didn't even chase after it."

"I agreed to be a tracker," Kama said. "Not a hunter."

"And I agreed to provide protection for your tracking services, not food. If you want to eat, you need to hunt. It's the price you have to pay for freedom."

"You call this freedom?" Kama asked. "You think humans are terrible for using food to get dogs to do what they want. Now you're doing the same thing."

Chapter 49

Dr. Bray walked up to the door. He glanced over his shoulder before swiping his identification card through a small box on the wall. A firm click sounded as the door bolt unlocked. Dr. Bray opened the door and closed it tight behind him. He walked down the hallway and entered a room.

"I thought I'd find you in here," he whispered.

"I just needed time to think," Shannon said.

The room was dark. Only one, dim lamp allowed him to see Shannon moving forward and back in a rocking chair. She was holding a bottle for the baby that was swaddled in her arms.

"I hadn't told Johnny about Purple Pup," she continued. "I was hoping they'd find him, that I wouldn't have to."

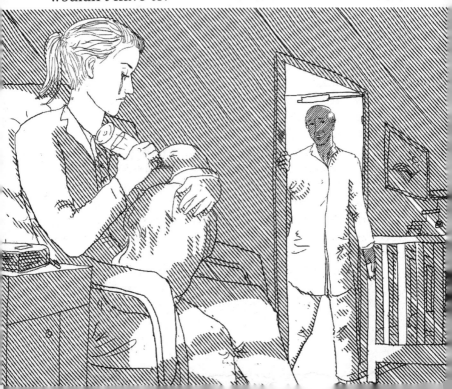

"But you told him now?" Dr. Bray asked.

Shannon nodded. A tear ran down her cheek.

Dr. Bray ran a hand across his shinny head. "I heard about Lieutenant Kimbal," he said.

Shannon sniffed and tried to blink the water out of her eyes. "Now that our funding is gone, our entire future depends on the Pet Shop. We'll be bankrupt in less than a year if it fails."

"It won't," Dr. Bray said.

This made Shannon smile. "Well, I'm glad one of us is optimistic." She stood up, walked across the room, and set the infant into a crib.

"Look, I know people don't like us right now, and that's a problem, but they're going to love our animals," Dr. Bray said.

"Don't like us," Shannon repeated. "They hate us. Activists are trying to shut us down, even before we've opened, and soon Johnny's family is going to tell everyone that we not only confiscated Purple Pup but also lost him."

"That's just it," Dr. Bray said. "Purple Pup is a great example. People are furious that we took him from Johnny. They all know he loves that dog."

"And your point is?"

"He loves that dog. Everybody does," Dr. Bray said, "and they're going to love our other animals too. The reason people don't like us is because everything we've done has been kept a secret."

"And for good reasons."

"But not any longer," Dr. Bray insisted. "Now we need people to support us. We need people to love Genetic Valley. They need to care about our research as much as the animals we create."

"We need a new public image," Shannon said.

Dr. Bray smiled. "Exactly."

Chapter 50

Daniel's muscles tightened. He crouched low to the ground. A rabbit was not far away. It hopped closer and lowered its head to nibble grass. Daniel sprang forward. He ran as fast as he could, but not quick enough. The rabbit darted beyond his reach and under a stone.

Daniel trotted to the hole the rabbit had slipped into. He was small enough to fit into the tunnel too, but he debated if he should. The tunnel was dark, too dark for him to see.

"Come on, don't be a scaredy-cat," Daniel mumbled to himself.

He was just about to crawl further inside when he heard a faint howl. Soon, the whole pack was howling, which was unusual for that time of the evening. Daniel backed his way out of the hole, so that he could listen more closely.

That's when the hairs on his back rose. Daniel could smell a creature he had never smelled before. He turned in time to see a raccoon charging at him. Daniel ran as fast as he could, but the sound of the creature's snarling was getting closer.

Daniel stopped near a log. He puffed up his mane and turned to face his attacker.

The raccoon stopped. It flashed its sharp teeth and the skin behind its nose wrinkled every time it hissed. Finally, it lunged forward, but stopped once Daniel lifted his paw. It tried to circle to the side before attacking again. This time it wasn't a bluff.

Daniel twisted his body away from the creature's mouth. He shrieked and the creature screeched. The two scuffled and swatted. Finally, the raccoon sunk its teeth into Daniel's shoulder. It shook its head violently and threw Daniel to the ground. Daniel wanted to get back up again but knew there wouldn't be time. He prepared to defend himself while laying down, but to his surprise the creature wasn't even looking at him.

Daniel heard a noise behind him. It was Congo, standing on top of the log, beating his chest rapidly with his fists. Congo jumped off the log and positioned himself in front of Daniel. The raccoon took a few steps backward, but it quickly realized that it was a little bigger than this second animal too. It flashed its teeth and attacked.

Chapter 51

After everyone had returned to the den, Nanook stood before the pack.

"Tonight, we have much to celebrate. Not only has Cryp proven himself to be an invaluable tracker, but he has shown us that he is strong, fast, and a natural hunter."

The wolves yelped in agreement.

"Can anyone remember the last time someone took down a full-grown deer on their first hunt?" Nanook asked.

Cryp proudly smiled as the wolves shook their heads and yelped even louder.

"Cryp, it is my honor to declare you a hunter, and as leader, I would like to offer you a permanent membership in this pack."

The wolves gasped and whispered as they waited for Cryp to say something.

Cryp was as shocked as the others. He wasn't sure what to say. He saw Kama's worried face. He also noticed the wolves anxiously wagging their tails, and, in particular, Tehya smiling. He couldn't remember the last time he had felt like this before. He realized he had never felt this way. For the first time, his life seemed to be exactly as it should be.

Cryp smiled. "Why, who could turn down an offer like that," he finally said.

The pack rushed forward. Cryp playfully jumped, nipped, and wrestled with them as they celebrated. Nanook was the only wolf who didn't crowd around Cryp. Instead, he threw his head back and howled. Eventually, the others howled too.

As their voices gradually faded away, Cryp's ears perked up. Kama's lifted higher too. A moment later, Cryp and Kama bolted into the forest.

Chapter 52

Congo jumped back onto the log. The raccoon followed him a distance, but soon lost interest. It turned around and focused on Daniel again.

By now Daniel was back on his feet. He hobbled away as fast as his injured shoulder allowed. He had no choice but to face the raccoon once more. This time, the raccoon seemed to have more confidence. It didn't slow down or show any sign of caution as it charged at Daniel. The two scuffled on the ground. The raccoon quickly rolled back onto its feet. It was about to dive at Daniel a second time, but its body was pulled backward.

Congo held the raccoon's tail. He tried to pull it even further away from Daniel. The creature instinctively spun around to protect itself, and Congo was knocked to the ground.

The animal was distracted, so Daniel leaped forward and sunk teeth deep into the raccoon's ear. It shrieked and flailed wildly. Despite being whipped from side to side, Daniel did his best to scratch at the animal's face. When he was flung to the ground, it wasn't because he let go of the creature. A small piece of its ear had completely ripped off.

Daniel saw rage in the creature's eyes as it rushed at him. It would accept nothing less than killing him to get revenge. Daniel braced himself, expecting to be overtaken by the creature's fury.

Suddenly, the raccoon was swept away by a flash of green fur. Cryp seemed to have bolted out of nowhere. Now that he had knocked the raccoon away, he chased the creature into the forest. Kama was not far behind. The chase did not last long though. The raccoon climbed the first tree it could, leaving the two dogs circling and barking below.

Lav and the wolves arrived a moment later.

Congo, not feeling comfortable with so many canines nearby, ran to a tree and climbed.

"Did you all see that," one of the wolves shouted. "This guy is awesome."

The wolf was referring to Cryp, who stopped barking at the raccoon and rejoined the pack.

"No kidding," another wolf said. "He can smell, he can take down a deer, he can fight. He's the greatest thing that ever happened to this pack."

Nanook quickly stepped in front of the others. "Well done Cryp. Why, you're just full of surprises aren't you?"

"I like to keep things interesting," Cryp said.

"Showoff," Tehya whispered.

Cryp stepped around Nanook and closer to Daniel. "Are you alright little guy?" he asked.

Daniel wasn't sure what to make of Cryp's question. After all, it was just a few days ago that the dog had wanted to tear him apart. Finally, he realized the question was sincere.

"Could be worse," Daniel said. He moved his shoulder and winced. "Don't worry,' He said, through clenched teeth. "I'll be the king of the jungle again in no time."

"No you won't," Congo said, from the tree branches. He spoke in a soft but stern voice. "You don't belong in this forest."

Daniel's ears gradually drooped.

"Yea," Kama said. She glared at Cryp then walked by him. "None of us belong here."

Kama walked toward den, and Lav trotted to catch up to her. Slowly, everyone else followed too.

Chapter 53

Mrs. Kantner was in her office. The usual sound of nearly a hundred keystrokes a minute abruptly stopped. Her fingers continued to rest on the keypad, but her eyes were focused on the pencil lying on the desk. It wobbled back and forth.

The floor rumbled. There was a jolt. The computer screen went dark. The room shook. Drawers filled with papers and folders slid open. Soon the whole filing cabinet toppled over.

She crawled under the desk and covered her head. Ceiling tiles fell and walls cracked. Mrs. Kantner screamed as the entire building collapsed.

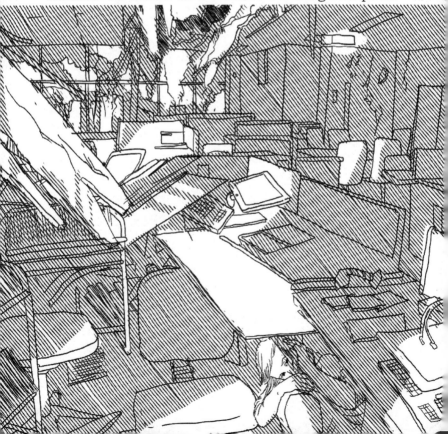

Chapter 54

Shannon waited until most of the workers left for the evening, before going to Dr. Bray's office. "I need a sedative," she said, closing the door behind her. "For something that weighs six kilograms."

Dr. Bray remained in his chair. His face was stern. "You should tell people."

"And go to prison?"

"That was always a possibility," Dr. Bray said. He crossed his arms. "You knew that."

"I thought people would understand," Shannon said. "I thought that once they learned about the advancements we've made with the Pet Shop, they would be more accepting of human modifications."

"They'll go easier on you if you turn yourself in."

Shannon shook her head. "Please, help me."

Dr. Bray stared at her. Finally, he stood and unlocked a medicine cabinet. He took out a small bottle and put on gloves. "This will make something that size sleep for a few hours." He filled a syringe with medication and handed it to Shannon.

She put the syringe into the side pocket of her lab coat. "Thank you," she said, before leaving.

Once down the hallway, Shannon slid her identification card through the small box on the wall. She entered the nursery, turned on the lamp, and went to the crib.

The infant was awake. Shannon washed her hands and took out a small plastic container from a drawer. The infant cooed and waved its arms, as it was picked up. Shannon sat in the rocking chair. Now that they were closer to the lamp, a yellow light reflected from within the baby's eyes.

Shannon opened the plastic container. She picked up one of the contact lenses that was inside and forced the baby's eyelid up. The infant squirmed in her lap while she put the lens in place. Only one of the baby's eyes continued to glow, until Shannon inserted the second contact.

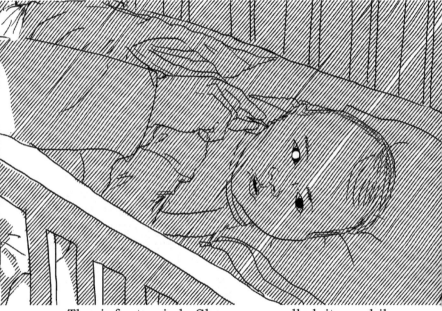

The infant cried. Shannon cradled it a while, before removing the syringe from her pocket. She uncapped the needle and injected the medication into the baby's thigh. The infant screamed, but not very long. Soon the crying stopped. Its body grew limp, and it fell into a deep sleep.

Shannon strapped the baby into a car seat. She hid the seat inside of a large box, before carrying it down the hallway, out of the laboratory, and eventually to the back seat of her car.

Chapter 55

Dana stopped in front of a large wooden door. She stood as tall as she could, took a deep breath, and knocked just below the brass plate that had "Commander Nelson" engraved on it.

"Come in," a voice immediately answered.

Dana opened the door and stepped inside.

"You wanted to see me sir?"

"Yes, come in, and close the door behind you."

To Dana's surprise, Commander Nelson was not alone. Lieutenant Kimbal was also there, which was just as unusual as being called to the commander's office so late in the evening.

Questions began to race through her mind. *Do they think I had something to do with Kama and Cryp running away? Are they blaming me for the failures at Genetic Valley?*

"Please have a seat," Commander Nelson said. He gestured to a chair beside Lieutenant Kimbal, but continued talking before she even had a chance to sit down. "It's my understanding that you have been working closely with Kama for over a year now. Is that correct?"

Dana nodded, as she lowered herself into the seat. "Yes sir."

"Then I presume that you have a better understanding of Kama and her abilities than anyone else."

Dana glanced at Lieutenant Kimbal. "That's right sir."

"Good." Commander Nelson put his hands behind his back and looked out the window. "Dana, in your expert opinion, is Kama prepared to take on the duties she has been trained for."

"Of course," Dana said. "She's exceeded all of her goals months ago."

The commander nodded as he stepped away from the window. "So I've heard."

"Sir, may I ask what this is about?" Dana asked.

Commander Nelson stroked his beard and sat down in the large chair behind his desk. His eyes appeared distant. Although they occasionally moved, they did not look at anything in particular. Finally, his eyes seemed to focus again. This time he was looking right at her.

"Due to unfortunate circumstances, we have a renewed interest in Genetic Valley's canine program," Commander Nelson said, "which is why I'm giving you new orders to find the missing dogs as soon as possible. Lieutenant Kimbal will be in charge of organizing a search team."

Commander Nelson stood up from his seat. Dana and Lieutenant Kimbal quickly did the same.

"You are to report to the base first thing in the morning," the commander continued, "the pilots will be waiting for you."

"Pilots," Dana repeated.

Chapter 56

Shannon drove deep into the city before parking on the side of an empty street. Only then did she remove the car seat from the box. Shannon leaned close to the sleeping baby. She kissed its forehead. Tear drops trickled off her cheek. She caressed its tiny fingers. "I'll always love you," she said.

A black van pulled up on the other side of the road. Twice its headlights turned off then on. Shannon wiped her tears away, and then flashed her headlights too. A man and woman stepped out of the van. Shannon picked up the car seat and carried it to them.

"I had to use a sedative to sneak her out," Shannon handed the car seat to the man. "She'll wake up in a couple hours."

The man turned the car seat so that his wife could see the baby.

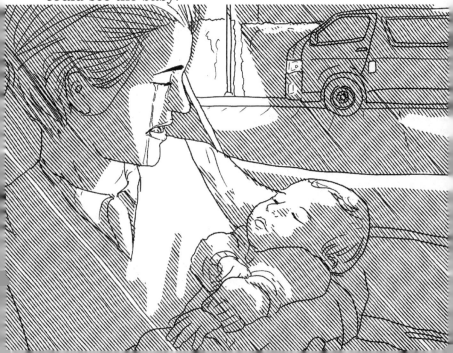

"She's so precious," the woman whispered.

Shannon nodded. "You have an amazing child."

"We can't thank you enough," the man said, as he carried the baby to their van. "It would have been impossible for us to have a healthy kid of our own. It's a shame we have to keep this a secret."

"I know," Shannon said. "Genetic defects shouldn't have to stop people from having children." She watched them fasten the car carrier onto the back seat. "Her contacts are in by the way. Make sure they stay in. Otherwise, people might suspect."

"We will," the woman said. She closed the back door. "At least until new laws are passed."

The couple returned to their seats. The van's engine started, and they drove away, leaving Shannon alone in the street.

Chapter 57

"Please, let me know as soon as you hear something."

Johnny could tell by the way his father was talking quietly into the phone that it was serious. Lexie could sense trouble too. She trotted over to the boy. She rubbed the side of her body against his leg until he picked her up.

"Thanks. You too," his father said, then hung up.

"They found him. Didn't they," Johnny said.

Johnny's dad shook his head. "That was your mom's company." He took a deep breath and ran a hand through his hair. "There was an earthquake in Ecuador—a couple hours ago."

"Is Mom alright?"

"Well nobody's sure right now. They've been trying to call her phone, but she hasn't answered."

Chapter 58

Cryp stood over a large set of tracks left in a muddy part of the woods. "What kind of deer made this?" he asked.

"Those are moose tracks," a wolf explained. "They don't often come to this part of the mountain."

"A moose, that's why they smell so different," Cryp said. "I bet they carry a lot of meat on them."

"Yea they're huge," Tehya said. "Last time we took one down, the pack was full for a week."

Cryp's tail wagged. "Well, what are we waiting for? Let's go."

"We don't hunt moose," Nanook said.

"But I thought you've taken them down before," Cryp said.

Nanook shook his head. "That was long ago. Moose are too dangerous. The scar on my face is proof of that. One kick, that's all it takes to kill a canine."

"I'm not afraid," Cryp said. "Come on, if you want a moose for dinner, follow me."

"I like the sound of that," another wolf said.

Half the pack raced after Cryp.

"No! Stop," Nanook shouted. He let out a deep growl. "Wait here," he told the others, before sprinting after the disobedient pack members.

Kama and Lav didn't listen though. They followed close behind him.

Cryp sniffed and trotted the path the moose had walked. Then his ears perked higher. He stopped.

"Is it close?" Tehya asked.

"No," Cryp said. "Be quiet."

Tehya and the others listened. "What is it?"

"I don't know."

Cryp stepped around a few trees, so that he could get a better view of the mountain. He seemed to be staring at the peak. "I haven't heard anything like it before."

"You all know the rule," Nanook said, when he finally caught up. "We don't hunt moose."

Kama's ears focused in the direction of the mountain peak too. "They're getting closer," She said, the sidestepped so she could be closer to Lav.

Slowly, the others began to hear a faint sound. The sound grew much louder as a camouflaged helicopter flew over the mountain's rim.

"What kind of bird is that?" Tehya asked.

"I don't know," Cryp said.

A second helicopter appeared, soon it turned and flew toward the canines.

Nanook leaped to the front of the pack. "Alright everyone, back to the den."

Chapter 59

"Bingo," the pilot said, "Look to your right."

At first, all Dana saw was an empty forest, but then a flash of purple caught her attention. She lifted a set of binoculars. "Purple Pup," she said.

He was mostly obscured, but now and then, he ran where there were gaps in the trees.

"Can you get us closer?" Dana asked.

"I'm on it," the pilot said.

The helicopter tilted to one side. A few minutes later, they were following a short distance behind Lav. As the pilot flew closer and closer to the tree tops, more of the wolves became visible.

"Looks like he made some friends down there," the pilot said.

"There she is," Dana shouted, "and Cryp too!"

After a while, the helicopter zoomed past the dogs. They were entering a small hole on the side of a hill. The helicopter circled back. A black wolf remained visible. It stared at them as they hovered.

"Can you get me down there?" Dana shouted.

"No can do," the pilot said. "We'll have to find a better place to land. Hold on a second."

The helicopter tilted to the side and sped away.

Chapter 60

The sound of the helicopter faded then vanished before Nanook finally entered the den.

Tehya was still trembling.

"It's going to be alright," Cryp said to her.

"Get out of here," Nanook growled. He squeezed his way through the pack and nipped at Cryp until he began to move.

Cryp backed away. "What's your problem?" he asked.

"You disobeyed me, tried to lead half of my pack on a dangerous mission, and brought these terrifying birds to the mountain," Nanook replied.

"You think the birds are my fault?" Cryp asked.

"Their colors and markings look just like you and Kama, and we've never seen them here before," Nanook said. "It's time for you to leave."

"Leave?"

"Leave now! All of you," Nanook shouted.

"Cryp, let's go." Kama said. She and Lav made their way to the den's entrance.

Cryp looked at Tehya, then at the other wolves. He shook his head. "I don't want to go."

"Come on Nanook," Tehya said. "He's the best thing that's happened to us in a long time."

"He's a domestic. He'll always be a domestic. It was a mistake trying to make him one of us," Nanook said. "Go back to where you belong."

Nanook growled and followed Cryp as he backed outside of the den.

Now that the helicopter was gone, Daniel poked his head out of a gap in the rock pile. He only glanced at the sky for a moment or two before he noticed how angry Nanook was. Daniel could sense trouble and scurried deep into the rock pile again.

Kama perked her ears higher as she left the den. There were voices. One was her trainer's voice. Kama knew Cryp could hear the voices too. "Cryp, it's time for us to go," she said.

"But I'm a member of the pack," he protested.

"Not any longer," Nanook snapped.

Cryp shook his head. "You can't do that."

"I'm the pack leader. I decide who's a member and who's not."

"Well, maybe it's time the pack chooses a new leader," Cryp said.

Nanook flashed his fangs. "Are you challenging my authority?"

"Yea, I am," Cryp barked.

Nanook held his head low to the ground. His nose wrinkled as he growled. The hair on his back rose and his eyes narrowed.

"You guys just calm down," Tehya said.

Nanook stepped closer to Cryp. "He's left me no choice. Either he leaves, or I'll kill him."

Chapter 61

Cryp crouched in anticipation of an attack. "I don't want to hurt you," he said, "but I'm not going anywhere."

"So be it," Nanook replied, and the two canines began circling each other.

"Cryp, that's enough," Kama said, but he ignored her.

"Don't fight," Tehya said. "Cryp, just go... Please go."

Cryp shook his head. "I belong here, with you."

Nanook lunged forward. The two canines snapped at one another and became a twisting, turning blur. Teeth flash and claws scratched as they tried to wrestle the other to the ground.

"Lav, do something," Kama said.

"Like what?"

Kama thought for a moment, and then darted into the forest.

"Kama," Lav barked. He chased after her.

"Stay here," she said, but Lav continued to follow. "Stay! I'll be right back."

Lav finally stopped.

Kama dashed through the forest. Every so often her trainer shout her name. Eventually, Kama thought she was close enough for the humans to hear her. "Over here. We're over here," she barked.

"Do you hear that?" one of the searchers asked.

Dana strained her ears. At first, she heard nothing but the breeze through the trees. Then she heard it. It was a dog barking.

"Kama," Dana yelled. After spending so much time with Kama, Dana easily recognized her bark. Dana whistled. The barks grew louder and louder. Eventually, she could hear something moving. "Kama, here girl," Dana said, then finally distinguished Kama's fur from the rest of the forest.

Kama stopped and barked again.

"Here girl."

The barking continued, but now Kama took a few steps backward.

"Something's wrong," Dana said. She jogged closer to Kama. "This isn't like her."

As they approached, Kama turned and trotted in the direction she had come from. Sometimes she seemed to wait for them, but most of the time all they could do was follow the sound of her barks.

Chapter 62

The fight was still going on when Kama returned. Both Cryp and Nanook were moving slower now. Both appeared to be in a great deal of pain. They frequently stopped to catch their breath before continuing the fight.

"Hey, do you guys hear that?" one of the wolves asked. "Does that sound like humans?"

"Your master is calling," Nanook teased, before beginning the next round of their battle.

"I don't have a master," Cryp snapped. "I've chosen to be wild."

They continued to bite at each other's necks. Cryp jumped forward and wrapped his front paws around the wolf. He was able to bite the side of Nanook's face long enough to give a strong tug.

Nanook stumbled and fell to the ground. He rolled onto his back and growled. When Cryp attacked, Nanook quickly twisted out of the way. The two canines seemed entwined as they tumbled across the ground. Each time one stretched out to bite, the other curved its body just out of reach.

It looked as if the struggle would last forever. Then Nanook bit deep into the skin under Cryp's throat. He thrashed his head back and forth. Cryp tried to fight Nanook off, even after he fell to the ground. It was no use though. Nanook was relentless. He lashed at Cryp's body over and over again.

"Stop it," Tehya cried.

Suddenly, there was a flash of purple, and Nanook was thrown to the side. Lav stood in front of Cryp, and Kama quickly joined him.

Nanook sprang to his feet but did not attack. He looked exhausted. His pack members gathered behind him. "Get out of the way or we'll kill all of you," Nanook warned.

"Yea, no interfering," another wolf said. "The fight is between Nanook and Cryp."

"The fight is over," Kama barked. "He'll be lucky if he survives."

"That's the way of the wild," Nanook said, but he took a few steps backward.

Nanook's ears, and everyone else's, were focusing on the humans. They could hear loud shouts and the snapping of twigs beneath boots.

"I want you off our mountain. You're no longer welcome here," Nanook said, then turned to his pack. "Let's go everyone. It's time for us to leave."

Nanook limped as he trotted away. The other wolves followed, quickly concealing themselves in the forest, except for Tehya. She followed Lav and Kama closer to Cryp.

"Tehya," Cryp whispered, between gasps for air.

"I'm right here."

Cryp lifted his head, as if he wanted to stand.

"Stop," Tehya said. "You need to rest."

Tehya laid on the ground. She nuzzled close to Cryp until the side of her face was touching his. Gradually, Cryp's breathing relaxed.

Chapter 63

Congo climbed down from a tree. He ran over to the rock pile. "Time to go."

Daniel squirmed his way out from the stones.

"Hurry, before the wolves return," Congo said.

The two minis made their way toward the sound of human voices. Daniel ran the best he could with an injured shoulder. Eventually, they saw people in camouflaged uniforms walking through the forest.

Daniel stopped when he realized Congo was no longer following. "Come on, let's get out of here."

Congo shook his head. "I'm not going with."

"What are you talking about? We can't stay here."

"You can't stay here," Congo corrected. "You've struggled to catch food and you're vulnerable to predators. I climb trees and have pine nuts to eat."

"Are you serious," Daniel asked.

Congo nodded. "I'll miss you my friend."

The humans were getting closer to where Cryp was lying.

"Do you see that? A wolf," someone yelled.

"Hold your fire," Dana shouted, "You might hit the dogs."

Daniel glanced at the humans. Then ran back to Congo and wrapped his paws around him.

Chapter 64

Tehya stood when humans emerged from the forest.

"Wait," Cryp said, before trying to lift his head again. He whined and squeezed his eyes closed, as if the fast movement had given him a blast of pain.

Tehya's body stiffened. Her eyes widened. She had never been so close to humans before and had definitely never allowed one to see her. "I have to go," she said, without taking her eyes off the people.

"Tehya," Cryp begged, but she took a few steps away from him.

"I'm sorry," she said, then dashed out of sight.

"Tehya," Cryp called. He whimpered a few more times while trying to lift his head. Then he closed his eyes, and they stayed closed.

"Cryp," Kama barked. She nudged him with her nose.

Cryp winced, but still didn't say anything.

"Kama, here girl" Dana called.

Kama wagged her tail. She turned and bounded into her trainer's arms.

"Good girl. I missed you so much."

Lav was surprised at how happy Kama looked. Dana looked happy too. She gave Kama a hug and rubbed the fur behind her ears. Then Dana stopped petting Kama and did something a little unusual. She leaned close to Kama, looked her right in the eyes, and said, "No more of this running away nonsense. A lot of people need your help."

Someone approached Lav with a collar and leash. He backed away and growled.

"Knock it off," Kama scolded. She followed her trainer back to the helicopter. "I think something is wrong. My trainer has never talked to me like that."

Lav couldn't help it. He didn't trust the humans and certainly didn't want to go back to the Valley. "But we need to find the boy," he whined.

"Come on Lav," Daniel called, as he emerged from the forest. "Do you really want to be here when the wolves come back?"

Lav finally calmed down. A human carefully placed the collar around Lav's neck. Then he pulled a phone out of his pocket and dialed a number.

"Hey Shannon, you can start contacting Johnny. We've got Purple Pup."

Chapter 65

Lav couldn't decide what the most terrifying experience of his life was; being locked in the cold, dark, moving room the first time he escaped from the Valley, or riding in the belly of the loud, flying bird. All he knew for sure was that he was glad when the bird landed by the laboratory and he could hop onto the ground again.

Someone led Lav away from the flying bird. Its deafening sound finally softened. That's when he heard Johnny's voice.

"Purple Pup!"

Lav glanced at the group of people waiting outside by the laboratory. His eyes focused on the shortest person in the group. He tugged so hard against his leash that he practically pulled the man hanging on to it over to Johnny.

"I was afraid I wouldn't see you again boy."

Johnny gave Lav a hug, the same way Kama's trainer had given her one. That's when Lav realized he didn't know where Kama was. Daniel was in a small pet carrier, not too far away. Cryp had been placed on a stretching board, and a few people were carrying him to the laboratory. Finally, Lav noticed Kama and her trainer were still inside of the large bird.

"What are you doing?" Lav barked. "Come here."

Kama stared at him. A short while later the bird lifted from the ground. Lav continued barking as it carried Kama into the sky. Its loud noise became faint as it shrunk into the horizon.

"Johnny. Just the boy I've been looking for. I have a proposition for you." Shannon said.

Johnny continued to pet Lav, refusing to acknowledge her as she waked closer to them.

"With all the chaos going on around here lately, we've been getting a bad reputation in the media. A lot of people want to shut this place down." Shannon gestured to the crowd of protesters by Genetic Valley's archway. "Our grand opening is just a week away, and we really need it to go well. We're hoping you could help us out."

"Me?" Johnny asked.

Shannon knelt on one knee beside him. "You love Purple Pup. Don't you?"

Johnny nodded.

"Well, I want every child to fall in love with the animals we've made, just like you've fallen in love with Purple Pup. I'm going to discuss the details with your father, but I want you to make some public appearances with Purple Pup and promote our research. In return, he can live with you."

Johnny grinned.

"It'll be scary though," Shannon warned. "I'm talking about television interviews and large crowds. Is this still something you're interested in?"

Johnny looked at his father. "Can I?"

Mr. Kantner had dark bags under his eyes. Johnny's grin faded. For a moment, he had forgotten that his mother was still missing. His father's tired stare was a reminder. Johnny too had laid awake most of the night worrying about her.

Mr. Kantner forced a smile. He gave a slight nod.

"Alright, but this is going to be a secret," Shannon said. "Let's go inside and talk more."

Chapter 66

There were dozens, maybe close to a hundred search dogs sniffing the rubble. All eyes were on Kama though. None of them had known a camouflaged dog even existed.

"We've gone over that area a day and a half already. It's clear," someone yelled to Dana. "Come help with a different zone."

Dana ignored the person and all the other comments they were receiving. "Focus Kama, this is your chance to shine. This is what you've been training so hard for."

Kama carefully felt the rubble with her paw to see if it was safe to step on. It was slow, hard work to climb the mangled pieces of collapsed building, but she kept moving. She could smell someone.

A layer of dust collected on Kama's fur as they climbed higher up the mess. The smell was getting stronger. Where was it coming from though?

She smelled gaps and openings in the twisted pieces of iron. Finally, she found one openings was emitting the strongest odor. She layed next to it.

"Good girl," Dana said, before shouting to the rescue workers. "Over here. We found one."

"Are you sure?" a man called back.

Kama's ears twitched. Something was moving down the hole.

"*Help.*"

The voice was faint, too faint for her trainer to hear. Kama stood and barked.

"See, she's found someone," Dana shouted. "Get a crew over here. We need to clear these pieces."

Workers eventually came. They cut through the rubble and dug deeper into the fallen building.

"We've gone down quite a ways," the crew chief finally said. "Still nothing."

"Well keep going. I know there's someone there," Dana insisted. "Kama. Where are they? Find them."

Kama climbed into the pit the workers had cleared. She sniffed, making her way to one side. She scrapped at a piece of wood, then laid down.

"Dig over there," Dana said.

The chief shrugged. His workers pulled more pieces of wood out of the pit. The chief found a place to sit and rest his feet. Then one the worker stopped.

"Hello," the worker shouted. He bent so his ear was be closer to the ground. The worker stood back up. "Someone's asking for help down there."

"Well I'll be," the chief said. He unclipped a walkie-talkie from his belt. He held the device over his mouth. "We need more hands in sector seven. Send a couple jacks with too."

Dana whistled, and Kama rose to her feet. "Alright Kama, let's look for more."

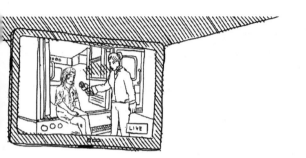

Chapter 67

Johnny's grandmother fell asleep to the repetitive sounds of her heart monitor's, "beep, beep, beeping" and the weatherman, on the 8 o'clock news, talking.

"Monday will be partly cloudy, with a slight chance of rain later in the evening..."

She still held onto the television remote. It was slowly slipping out of her hand.

"Hello, I'm Sophia Gral," a reporter said. We're interrupting the weather report for just a moment to update you on breaking news emerging from the earthquake's epicenter."

Footage of Kama and Dana appeared.

"Rumors of a camouflaged hero have just been confirmed. Her name is Kama. Just like Purple Pup, she was created in Genetic Valley. What's special about Kama though, is that she seems to have one powerful sniffer."

The video zoomed in and focused on Kama holding her nose close to the ground. Then she laid down, and Dana waved for help.

"Records show that Kama found seven missing people today, some of which had not been detected by other search dogs. Not bad, considering this is Kama's first search and rescue mission."

A video of Mrs. Kantner appeared on the screen. She sat in the back of an ambulance. The dark gray suit she wore looked tan, because she was covered with so much dust. Her hair was messy, and she had cuts and busies on her face.

The reporter held a microphone in front of Mrs. Kantner's Mouth. "It was completely dark. I didn't think I would ever get out. Then I heard a dog barking. That was the first hope I had in two days. The workers said that without Kama, I wouldn't have been found."

The remote control dropped from the grandmother's hand. She took her last breath.

"beep, beep, beep, beep, beeeeeeeeeeeeeeeeeee..."

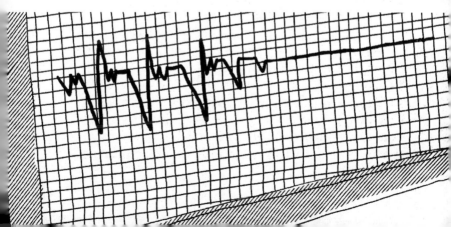

Chapter 68

Kama wasn't sure where they were going. It was a part of the laboratory she had never seen before.

"Cryp," Kama barked, when she detected his scent. "Are you alright? Cryp?"

"Hey, take it easy," Dana said. "They just need your DNA, then you'll never have to come back here again."

Cryp's scent grew stronger, but he didn't reply to her barks. Finally, a couple men appeared. They were pushing a medical bed down the hallway.

"How did the procedure go?" Dana asked.

"Lickity-split," a man said. "They're all set up for Kama in the ultrasound room."

Kama looked at the bed as it was wheeled by. She began to whine when she saw Cryp lying on top. Although it looked like the wounds from his fight were healing, his eyes were closed.

"Don't worry. He'll wake up in a little while," Dana said. "Now it's your turn."

"Could you have her hop onto the bed?" Dr. Bray asked, once they arrived. He wore a surgical mask and gloves, just like the others in the room.

Dana hoisted Kama from the ground and set her on a bed that looked identical to the one Cryp had been on. Dana also sat on the bed to comfort Kama.

"How many surrogates are there going to be?" Dana asked, after she accepted a mask from one of the workers and tied the strings behind her head.

Dr. Bray shook his head. "That depends."

"On what?"

"Many things. In-vitro is harder with dogs than with people. Everything has to be just right for the embryo to survive." Dr. Bray walked to them with a needle and squirted a small stream of medication into the air. "But if this first collection goes well, there might be enough for three litters."

Dana smiled and scratched the fur behind Kama's ears. "You hear that Kama. There might be three mothers having puppies for you and Cryp."

Dr. Bray leaned closer to Kama. "Alright, you're going to feel a little poke."

The needle entered Kama's leg. She flinched, but the pain didn't last long. Her body felt weak. Kama laid her head on Dana's lap and fell asleep.

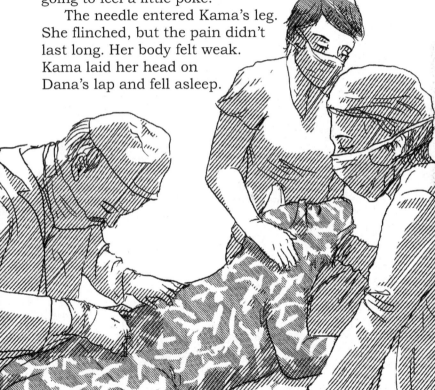

When Kama woke up she was in the dog room. She could tell by the dim light coming through the window that it was late in the evening.

"Hey look who's awake," one of the dogs teased. "You almost slept as long as Lav did."

"Lav was here?" she asked.

"For a little while. A couple days ago, him and Violetta were sleeping a lot, just like you and Cryp. Once he woke up, that boy took him away."

Kama slowly sat up. She looked into Cryp's kennel. He was lying on the floor.

"I've been worried sick about you," she said.

Cryp didn't respond.

"Cryp?"

He finally stood up and walked to the other end of his kennel. He laid down again but made sure he was facing away from everybody.

"Don't take it personally," one of the other dogs said. "He hasn't been talking to anyone."

"Where were you guys?" another dog asked. "Is Lav coming back?"

"Sorry, I'm still kind of tired," Kama said. She laid back down.

"Man, running away made you guys boring."

Kama was tired, but that wasn't the only reason she didn't answer their questions. She didn't know all the answers either, like if they would see Lav again. She was wondering the same thing herself.

Suddenly, there was a noise. Somewhere in the distance, a wolf was howling. Kama could tell by the way Cryp's ears twitched that he heard it too. It was Tehya's howl.

"You were right Kama," Cryp finally said.

Kama lifted her head. "About what?"

"Me and you," he muttered, "we never did love each other."

There were footsteps in the hallway. Kama sniffed the air. It was her trainer.

Dana entered the room and unlatched Kama's kennel. "Alright girl, say goodbye to everyone," she said. "From now on, you're living with me."

Chapter 69

Shannon walked up the stairs. Her hair was not in the usual ponytail but hung down past her shoulders. She stepped up to a microphone stand and looked at the crowd that had gathered. Behind her was a large set of doors. Their brass handles were connected by a thick, red ribbon.

Shannon leaned closer to the microphone. "Welcome to Genetic Valley, where creatures of the imagination come to life."

She blinked as dozens of camera flashes lit up the stage. "For many years now, we have been working hard to modify our animals in ways never done before. In a short while, you will see for yourself the remarkable results we have achieved."

Some crowd members began to applaud, forcing Shannon to wait before continuing. "Unfortunately, in the race to alter DNA, it's easy to belittle the lives that are made. The living things you'll see in a moment are just that. They're living animals, each with their own distinct personalities and desires."

Shannon gave a slight nod. A moment later, Johnny led Lav to the top of the steps.

"Like Purple Pup for instance," Shannon said. "He's showed us that even a purple dog has a desire to be man's best friend. And the many animals that escaped from our facility a few weeks ago, they have proven that even modified creatures have an inherent desire to be free."

"These recent events have reminded me that animals are not just meant to serve people, to make us happy. We have the responsibility to care for them too. To give them respect and dignity. To love them for the unique individuals they are.

"With this in mind, it's my honor to announce that Purple Pup has been given to Johnny Kantner, and he has agreed to live up to this responsibility."

Johnny couldn't help but to blush and smile as the crowd clapped. He stepped to the side, as Dr. Bray came forward with a large pair of golden scissors, which was handed to Shannon.

"Now without further ado, I present to you, Genetic Pet Shop." Shannon snipped the ribbon. She and Dr. Bray each grabbed one of the brass handles. Together, they opened the doors, making the animals available for everyone to see.

Chapter 70

Jim wore khaki pants and a dress shirt. His hair was neatly combed. He carried a small pet carrier as he followed an old man and a white-haired woman into a mansion.

"I'm so glad you agreed to work for us," the woman said. "We couldn't find anyone else with experience working in Genetic Valley."

"Yes, you have a rare expertise in deed," the old man said. "And how long have you worked with fluffy?"

"I've known him since he was a cub," Jim said.

"Oh. Do you have pictures?" the woman asked, her hands shaking with excitement.

"No. Sorry ma'am."

"What a pity," she said. "Why, I would just love to see a mini cub."

"Yea, he was cute alright," Jim said, "but always had a feisty personality."

The old man raised an eyebrow. "Who Fluffy? I didn't think he had it in him."

Jim smiled and nodded his head. "I know you folks paid top dollar for him, but I think the reason Genetic Pet Shop auctioned this one first is because he has a history of causing problems."

"Oh, what rubbish." The woman said. "I'm sure Fluffy will be just a sweetheart."

Jim set the pet carrier down. He opened the door and waited. Finally, he reached inside.

A loud hiss came from within the cage. Jim quickly pulled his hand away. He picked up the back of the carrier and tilted it forward until Daniel slid out.

"What is this place?" Daniel asked.

He studied the massive room. Glass chandeliers hung from the ceiling. A soft rug padded his feet.

To Daniel's surprise, there was a huge portrait of him hanging on the wall. Beneath the painting was a large, red pillow. Daniel ran up to it.

The woman smiled and clasped her hands together when Daniel plopped down on the pillow. "Awe, look dear. Fluffy likes his bed."

A small golden bowl was not far away. It was full of something delicious smelling.

"I could get used to this," Daniel said. He rolled to his back and stretched his paws out. "I don't know how a place like this could be any better."

"Oh Cynthia, here kitty," the old man called. "Come meet our new family member."

Daniel heard jingling and sat up. It was coming from the banister stairway. A beautiful cat appeared at the top step. She had thick, curly hair, and a small bell dangled from her collar.

Daniel couldn't help but stare. "Meee-ow," he purred.

Chapter 71

Kama sat in a jeep, beside her trainer. They drove down a long dirt road. Eventually, they pulled up to a little house, next to a red barn, and hopped out of the vehicle.

"Lav," Kama barked, recognizing his scent.

A screen door opened and slammed. Lav and Johnny hurried down the porch steps.

"Kama, what are you doing here," Lav barked.

The two dogs nipped and leaped at each other.

"I don't know. My trainer brought me."

"Come on, you should meet the others," Lav said.

Lav and Kama ran to the barn. Johnny followed.

"Hey Spit-Shot, Daisy, I told you my stories of the laboratory are real..."

Johnny's parents came out of the house too.

"Why if it isn't the two heroes," Mr. Kantner said. "Welcome to our home!"

"Thanks. It's nice here," Dana replied. "I heard you all just moved in."

Mr. Kantner nodded. "It was my parents' place. We almost sold it when my mom passed away."

"We were living in the city because it was near my company's office," Mrs. Kantner explained, "but now that people are paying so much to interview Johnny and Purple Pup; we decided I can work from here instead, even if it doesn't pay as well."

"Besides, Purple Pup needs a lot more running room than the city had to offer," Mr. Kantner added.

"Purple Pup! Kama," Johnny yelled. He waved a worn tennis ball, then threw it across the yard.

Lav and Kama darted from the barn. Lav snatched the ball. Kama tried to steal it, but Lav returned it to Johnny, who threw it again.

"So why did you want to visit?" Mr. Kantner asked.

"Well, I was watching Johnny on the *Late Night Show*, and Kama started barking as soon as Purple Pup appeared on the screen. I've never seen her so excited before. She almost knocked over my television. It looked like she missed him, so I decided to give you a call."

"Well they certainly do have fun together," Mrs. Kantner said, as Kama beat Lav to the ball this time.

A cell phone rang.

"Sorry, I need to take this." Dana said. She raised the phone to her ear and stepped away.

"You're right, fetch is awesome," Kama said. She had a big doggy grin on her face.

"I knew you'd like it," Lav said. "This is how I always imagined things would be if you were here. Everything is perfect."

"Kama," Dana yelled, before whistling loudly.

"It's time for me to go," Kama said.

"Go? Why? Stay here with me and the boy."

Kama shook her head. "You were right Lav. We really are meant to serve people. The boy is your person and my trainer is mine. I make her happy and she loves me, just like the boy loves you."

Another whistle shrieked across the farmyard. "Kama, now!"

"Hopefully we can play fetch again," Kama said, before dashing away.

Dana sat down in the jeep and started the engine. "That was my lieutenant on the phone. There's a missing boy in the city. He might have been kidnapped. The police want to see if Kama can help track him down."

The door slammed shut after Kama hopped into the vehicle. She stuck her head out of the passenger window. Kama and Lav barked to one another as the jeep sped down the dirt road.

Although Lav was disappointed that Kama was not going to stay, he was the happiest he had ever felt. He had lived at the farm before and had lived with the boy before. Only one thing had changed. Now he knew that Kama was safe and happy, and he had a feeling they would see each other again.

Chapter 72

Cryp's wounds continued to heal. Eventually, Dr. Bray decided Cryp had enough strength to resume his training. Dr. Bray was right too. Cryp did have enough strength. The moment they stepped out of the laboratory, Cryp lunged forward, pulling the leash right out of his trainer's hand.

Cryp sprinted across the valley. He knew exactly where he was going. He followed her scent all the way to the edge of the pine trees. That's where he was greeted by a wolf.

Despite another massive search, Cryp was never seen again, but after some months passed, reports indicated that a second wolf pack had established itself on the far side of the mountain range.

Ever since, there have been rumors of strange, green, wolf-like creatures living in that area.

The End

To the Reader:

May you find a place where you belong.

To Seth Godin:

I could have made Lav any color,
but chose purple as a tribute to *Purple Cow*.
Thanks for sharing your wisdom.

ISBN: 978-163578-001-7
First Edition

Current contact information for Karl Steam can be found at
www.karlsteam.com

Interior Illustrations
By: Joshua Lagman

Story and Cover Art
By: Karl Steam

Real-Life Modifications

GloFish were the first genetically modified (GM) pet to be approved by the U.S. Food and Drug Administration. They were invented in 1999 when researchers forced a gene that allows jellyfish to glow green into the embryos of zebrafish. The result was florescent green zebrafish.

GloFish

Since then, a couple different species of fish have been used to create GloFish, and they are available in many different florescent colors. It's too bad the pages for this book are printed in black and white. Now you'll never be able to see the spectacular colors of these fish. Mwahahaha!

Just kidding. You can go to my website, www.karlsteam.com, to watch videos of GloFish and to learn about other plants and animals that have been genetically modified.

GM Food

Chances are, you will eat GM food today. For decades, fruits, vegetables, and grain crops have been modified to grow better. Their DNA has been changed to make them more resistant to things like frost, drought, insects, and infections. They have been genetically modified to grow bigger, faster, and to survive longer.

The U.S. Department of Agriculture reported that in 2016, about 90% of all corn and soy beans grown in the United States were genetically modified. These crops are shipped throughout world, and will become ingredients in many of the food products you likely eat.

In 2015, the AquAdvantage Salmon became the first GM animal approved by the U.S. Food and Drug Administration to be sold as food in the U.S. This salmon has been modified to grow to its adult size twice as fast as regular Atlantic salmon do.

Is GM Food safe to eat? That depends, but it would take a while to explain, and don't even get me started on the labeling issues. Watch this video if you want to know more. It highlights some of the controversies involved with GM foods and can be viewed on YouTube or www.karlsteam.com.

Purple Pup was Karl Steam's first novel. He's since published the *Kids vs. Nature* series, an entertaining mixture of danger, adventure, and life lessons learned in the great outdoors. For a current list of books, please visit Karl's website.

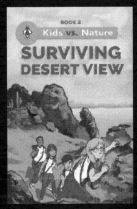

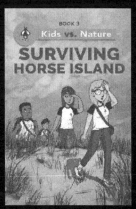

KARL STEAM.com

Made in the USA
Columbia, SC
10 December 2019